THE BONES OF ME

KEL DUCKHOUSE

FLYING EYE BOOKS

First edition published in 2022 by Flying Eye Books,
an imprint of Nobrow Ltd. 27 Westgate Street, London, E8 3RL.

The Bones of Me © Kel Duckhouse, 2022

Cover Illustration by Tosin Akinkunmi
Design by Justin Moore
Printed and bound by CPI Group (UK) Ltd,
Croydon, CR0 4YY on FSC® certified paper.

MIX
Paper from
responsible sources
FSC® C107574
FSC
www.fsc.org

ISBN: 978-1-91434-303-2

www.flyingeyebooks.com
www.nobrow.net

For Jimi

BLOOD ON FIRE

When you step in that ring,
it all goes quiet.

The minute you put your foot
to canvas,
    you're all alone.
No one can save you,
    but you.

It's proper powerful.

It's like, even though
    you're gonna
    get punched,
nothing can hurt you.

    You're
    invincible.

    You're
    free.

    You're
    blood on
    fire.

The devil, God
and all his angels
can't get you there,
let alone the world.

It all just fizzes away
and, for once, life seems
    fair.
It's just you and them,

and, unlike in real life,
no matter where you
     was born,
     who you are,
what dolla' you got,
you can actually
     win.

you can properly
know what it's like
to be a champion.

To
     b—r—e–a–t–h–e.

When you master
your mind . . .
your body,
nothing can hurt
you no more.

Not parents.
Not Old Bill.
Not government.
Not being poor.

     Nothing.

You become – truly
          Unbreakable.
          Unstoppable.

               A fighter.

ALBERT'S

It was always pie, mash and liquor the day after one of Denny's fights. Albert's was our favourite. Their food was cockney perfection. Minced beef, not too much gravy, mash with lumps, and the greenest parsley liquor you ever saw.

'Pie and mash,' Mum would say, 'is food of the gods. That's why the recipe is a proper secret. *God only doles it out to those what is special.*'

Albert's was no frills.
Wooden benches,
grey tables, tiled walls.

A black-and-white photo
of Albert and his family
stood outside the shop,
had pride of place
on the back wall.

Behind the counter, a tatty banner.

It had been there my whole life.

Pie and mash was all they sold.
    Except jellied eels –
that only old people ate,
cos it looked like snot and smelled worse.

This was old school East End.

Not like those new fancy places
        going up all over,
crawling with hipsters
with funny haircuts,
eating avocado brunches,
        spending money
        like it was going out of business.

Albert's was packed, but we found a table near the counter. Denny picked his scabby knuckles. His bruised face was hard to look at. He'd won, but he was a mess.

My old man was getting the usual. Single pie for me, double for the adults. He was flirting with the old lady behind the counter.

'Cheers, love,' said Dad. 'Be lucky.' He always put on his charm mask in public, but Mum, Denny and I knew he hid under duvets at home, wanting to block out the world.

'You be lucky yourself, darling.' She grinned, showing her crusty teeth.

'Rory,' said Mum, giggling.

'Think I found a new admirer! What do you reckon, Molly?'

Even though I knew it was all an act, it felt nice to have him in a good mood. 'Not sure she'd have you, Dad.'

He doled out spoons and forks and sat down next to me. We all got ready to tuck in, except Denny.

I hugged my plate close and cut my pie in half with my spoon. You ain't meant to use a knife, unless you want to be a fake cockney, and no one wants that. I let the beefy juice mix with the liquor, then drowned it in vinegar.

'Wipe that cob off your face, son. Bit more training – the next one's brown bread.'

Denny bit his lip, looked at Mum. She smiled, put her hand on his.

'Too right, Den,' I said, through a gob full of pastry.

I wondered what it felt like, the day after a fight. Denny was black and blue, but still a champ. I'd risk a few bruises too, for five seconds in a boxing ring.

Denny shoved his plate away, crossed his arms.

'If you don't eat that, I will,' I said, needing noise.

Denny moved his plate closer to him. 'In your dreams, kiddo.'

I shoved the chilli vinegar across the table at him. I had normal on mine, but Denny preferred a bit of spice.

'Get you fixed up and back down the gym.' Dad chomped his pie. 'Old Sonny Marsten reckons he can get a fight up Bethnal Green.'

I imagined Dad planning *my* next fight. Me, in the ring, crowds roaring my name.

'Leave him, love,' said Mum, 'He's not well. Poor thing.' She wrapped her arm round his waist. Denny winced.

'You need to get back on it. Ain't that right, son?'

Denny ignored him, got up, went to the counter.

'You can't keep pushing him, Rory,' Mum whispered.

'Leave it, will you, love?' Dad put more vinegar on his pie.

'I don't like seeing him upset.'

Dad sighed.

Denny slid back into his seat.

Silence.

Again.

I dragged mash through the bright green liquor on my plate. Fell into a daydream. Me in the ring, knocking someone out, best female fighter in London, in the *world*, maybe. I shook my head, annoyed at letting myself dream something that'd never happen to some low-life girl from a council estate.

'Frank Tessie reckons he can get me a shot at a belt.'

Dad smacked his hands on his knees; our plates hopped on the table – *clang, clunk, slosh.*

'What does Frankie bleedin' Tessie know?'

Denny shook his head, pulled his lips tight.

'It's not working any more, Dad.'

'Don't be daft, Dennis,' said Mum, putting her hand on his leg. 'You're punch drunk. You ain't thinking right.'

Denny nudged Mum's arm off. 'I'm not punch nothing, Mum. I'm sick of fighting on the undercard. I've got a shot and I want to take it. Granddad believed in me – why can't you?'

'I do believe in you, son.'

The nosy old cow sitting across from us pretended not to look.

Mum hid her face behind her hand. 'We should go home,' she announced. 'A cuppa – that'll help, eh, boys?'

Denny leaned forward. 'You stopped believing in anything a long time ago.'

Solid silence.
    Its heaviness
    crushed the air around us.
Dad's lip trembled;
he looked away,
flopped into the bench,
    buried his face in his hands.
    'Do what you like. I give up.'

Dad rested his head on Mum's
shoulder. She nestled him,
combed his hair
with delicate fingers,
careful not to break him.

I pitied him.

Denny waved his hand at me.
    'Come on, kiddo, let's get out of here.'
I looked at Mum.
Made sure it was OK.
She nodded.
I didn't like leaving her,
but Dad's mood was suffocating.

UPSTART

Out on Green Street
the smell of warm pastry
gave way to the whiff of discarded
vegetables and pigeon mess.
The hollers of the Saturday market traders
    washed away the thought of Dad.
Denny lit a rollie, his hands shaking.
He took a drag.
His chest went big for a minute.
It seemed to calm his nerves.
    'I reckon it's about time we taught you to fight proper.'
I forced a confused look.
Pretended I hadn't the foggiest
what he was on about.
    'I don't want to fight. What you on about?'
His dimples dented his cheeks.
    'Yeah you do.'
He had
me proper.
    'How'd you know?'
    'I've seen that look in your eye
    when we play box.
    Hard to miss.'
I shook my head.
    'Nah. Dad won't like it.'
Denny tapped the side of his nose.
    'Don't worry. It'll be our little secret.'
I gandered at the yellow bulges on his face.
    'Do I get red gloves?'
Denny flicked my ponytail.
    'Whatever you want, kiddo.
    Anything for my little sister.'

A BOXER IS BORN

It's Friday evening, the day before my first ever competitive fight – the under-sixteen's East London tournament. Denny's been prepping me solid. I should be on top form, but I ain't. I know it and Denny does too.

'Molly, for Christ's sake, put your back into it,' Denny says with proper angry, stupid eyes. 'Your fight is tomorrow night. Focus!'

I look to the other side of the ring. Frank, Denny's coach, is stood bogging at us. *What is his problem?*

I jab,
> one-two,
>> one-two.

Denny glares back. Frank yanks his hat off, shakes his head, storms into his office, slams the door. Denny huffs.

'Straighten those wrists. Come on, Molly!'

I narrow my eyes.
> One-two,
>> one-two.

A voice inside me whispers,

You can't do it.

> You're going to lose.

>> *You'll look like an idiot.*

I can't shut it up.

'Focus! Dig deep. Where's the fire in your belly?'

Denny's voice rings through me till I feel fire burning inside me. He's never this hard on me. Never this mean. I hate letting him down.

I square up.
Try again.
One-two,
    one-two.
I

S
 T
 U
  M
 B
 L
 E.

'Ah, sod this, I'm going for a fag.'
His voice venom. Doesn't sound like my Denny.
I whack the punchbag. 'Fine. I don't need you anyway.'
Denny slams the door. I feel the other boxers' eyes piercing into me. All of them in their designer boxing gear and me in my supermarket-bought trainers. They must think I'm a joke. *I* think I'm a joke.

Them voices come again.

They're laughing at you.
    Low . . . life . . . wannabe.

I clench my teeth, steady my weight, punch hard.

One for Denny –
two for him being a massive git.

One for being born on an estate –
two cos I'm never getting out of this dump.

One for *you can't do it* –
    two for . . .

. . . It comes whispering back at me –
You can't do it,
    People like you never make it.
And now it's shouting –

    IT'S TOO HARD –
        GIVE UP!

Shut up. Shut up. Shut up!

B*am*   B*aam*   B*aaam*

Why can't skint people make it?

B*am*   B*aam*   B*aaam*

Who says I can't win?

I whack. I thump until . . .

B*am*   B*aam*   B*aaam*

. . . the anger in my head
turns to the fire in my belly
that everyone keeps going on about . . .

Until . . .

proper faint like . . .
I swear I hear

    I can.

With each punch, the voice inside grows

    s t r o n **G E R,**

until I swear words are

falling right out
of my actual mouth –

'Yeah . . .
    I reckon . . .
        I can.'

'That's more blinkin' like it.' I never even noticed Denny come back in.
Tiff's clapping her gloves together. 'You're on fire, girl!'
Even Frank has an impressed grin on his craggy, wrinkled face.
I stop pounding the punchbag. It swings back at me. Knocks me clean
off my feet. I'm on the floor. Denny laughs, a proper belly chuckle. I laugh
too. Not cos it's funny. Cos I'm relieved.
He ain't angry anymore.
'Come on.' Denny puts his hand out to me, pulls me back up. 'Let's grab
a takeaway, then get us an early night. Big day tomorrow. Your first fight! You
need your rest.'

I hide my gym bag in case Dad starts asking questions. He reckons boxing
is a dreamers' sport and I should concentrate on getting a job in a shop, cos
dreams are for suckers. I know he's right, but I enjoy it, so Denny and I keep
it a secret. Dad would only ruin it for me, so he can naff right off.
We're hanging out in the front room on the settee, telly on, eating our
stash. Vanilla milkshakes, chips with ketchup for me and chilli sauce for him.
He sticks on some weird show about sexy women on an island. His eyes
almost pop out of his nut. The chips are tasty as hell but they need more salt,
so I chuck some on.
I look over and the blend is soundo on the sofa and snoring like a pig, a
chip sticking out his gob.
No way am I letting him get away with that.
I grab my phone, take a photo.
What a bleedin' slob!

SCARPERED

I wake up, Denny's gone.
    Last night's takeaway wrappers
        are dumped round the sofa.

I check his room.

    Empty.

I send him a quick text.

Nothing back.

    Nada.

        Zilch.

Something feels funny in my tummy.
We was meant to be having one last training sesh,
before my big fight tonight.

Where is he?

I pack my bag and head to the gym.

He must have
gone early.

PANDEMONIUM

Duke's is buzzing with the Old Bill.

    Police tape surrounding the place.

        With my fight tonight,

            it has to be the absolute worst timing ever.

    And still

Denny's nowhere to be seen.

Kwaku my bestie rocks up.

    'What's going on?' I ask.

        'They found a bloke, proper beaten up, out back by the bins.

            Word is he's so bad he's been put in a coma.

            Feds are questioning Frank now.'

'Are you freaking kidding me?'

    I think about Denny, about how I ain't seen him today.

        'It's no one we know, is it?'

        Kwaku shakes his head. 'Nah, some random.'

Frank comes out, lights up a fag. Sees us standing there.

    'All right, girl – everything has hit the fan here, I'm afraid.

        Gonna have to miss your morning session, sorry.

        I'll be at your fight later. Right?'

I nod my head.

    A little shaky.

        Feel almost scared.

Something seems out of sorts.

    'You seen Denny?'

        Frank takes his hat off, ruffles his hair.

            'Nah, sorry. I gotta get back in.

            Ol' Bill ain't done with me yet.'

'Why don't we go for a run?

    Warm those muscles up.' Kwaku smiles.

        I shake my head, trying to knock the anxious thoughts away.

            'Good idea. Race ya!'

    I leg it,

Leave Kwaku and the blue lights behind me.

AWOL

The police tape is still up when I arrive back at Duke's for my fight, but the Old Bill are long gone. I don't want to think about it. I ain't seen the bloke, but my imagination's making me think of what a mess he might be in. *Was he beaten? Stabbed . . . ? Worse? Who did it? Why?* Something's nagging inside me, right in my gut. *Are we safe?*

And the timing. Denny's still nowhere to be seen.

Punters are piling into the boxing hall. It's fuller than normal. Frank reckons everyone's being proper nosy, trying to find out what happened with that bloke – Harry Wilson – who was found by the bins.

I gander the crowd, shake my head, shut the changing room door, relieved to shut the haunting feelings away on the other side.

'He still not here?' Frank's holding some tape and a headguard.

'No, but he will be.'

'We've got to wrap them hands, Molly. Time's getting on.' Frank's pretty upbeat, which is a bit weird, considering some geezer's been found half dead in his gaff only a few hours ago.

'He's probably missed the bus. I'll wait.'

'How about we just get started?' says Frank.

'Wrapping's Denny's job. He'll be here.'

I pace the room. *We ain't even weighed in yet.*

He still has time.

I grab my phone from my gym bag and message him.

> Hurry up will ya? ☹

Tiff puts her hand on my shoulder, her touch firm, the muscles in her arm tight. I wonder if I'll ever be as buff as her, cos I'm weedy as hell.

'What about a warm-up?' she says. 'Shadowing? Bit of skipping maybe?'

I can't say no, I think she's so cool.

'Fine.'

I push my left foot forward, line up my shoulders, twist my back foot out, toe to heel. I bounce. My knees feel strong, my toes light. I right jab, then left hook an imaginary opponent.

A bell rings outside for weigh-in.

I check my phone.

Nothing.

Frank grabs the wraps. 'Right, Molly, you're gonna have to let me wrap them or we're gonna run out of time.'

I huff.

'You ever used tape before?' he asks.

'No.'

'Right, well, it's the same as the wraps, but it's even more solid.'

'Whatever.' I check the clock. Five minutes to go. Denny won't miss my first fight. Something must have happened. What if he's been hurt too? I mean, *they ain't caught anybody yet.*

The door flies open behind me.

Finally.

'Den . . . ?'

It's Happy Boy Kwaku. 'It's proper exciting out there! News are here asking all sorts. It's like the movies.' He beams like everything's a bloomin' joke.

It's the last thing I need. If news shows inside Duke's, my old man will find out I've been boxing, and me and Denny . . . well, we'll be brown bread. I brush the idea away. Dad'd never watch the news anyway. I'm being paranoid.

'What you doing here?' I ask Kwaku.

'Charmed, I'm sure. I came to see you fight, didn't I?'

'I didn't ask you to.'

Kwaku gives Frank and Tiff a look as if to say, *What's her problem?*

Frank shrugs. 'Denny's not turned up. He'll be here, Molly, but Denny don't matter right now. You've got to get some bleedin' focus. Put all your energy into the fight. Got it?'

I huff. 'I can't get the thought of that bloke, Harry Wilson, out of my head. Is he gonna live? Who would mash someone's face up like that? Proper psychos!'

Kwaku purses his lips. 'Yeah, it's really freaky. How'd you find out who it was though?'

'I googled him, what else? It's called a phone?' I don't want to admit I've been obsessively looking for clues since it happened.

'OK, calm down.'

Frank shakes his head, frustration plastered across his mug. 'Look, never mind all that. I'm sure the bloke will make a swift recovery and they'll find the man what did it to him. It'll be tomorrow's chip paper – nobody's gonna remember it in a few days' time.' He chucks my brand-new red gloves at me. 'Get those on your mitts.'

'Woah, they're a bit flashy!' Kwaku tries grabbing them for a better look.

'Coming from you, Mr Poser?' I snap. 'Denny bought them for me.' I pull my gloves away, shove them on.

'You ready?' Tiff opens the door.

The crowd outside's bigger. They aren't there to see me though. I'm just on the undercard of the proper pro fights later on. Nobody, not even Denny, is here to see me. Just stupid Kwaku and Frank and Tiff. Nobody who knows me properly will be here cheering me on.

Frank grabs me by my arms and shakes me.

Cheeky git. He looks at me, proper serious.

'Right, listen up, missy. When you lay that first foot on the canvas, go through those ropes and that second foot lands – you're in there alone. You've got to believe, Molly. No doubts. Ultimate faith. Put everything else out your head and focus. Ain't no one else gonna help you in there, but you. Got it?'

I nod. Maybe he's right. Maybe a kid like me can do it. Be a somebody. Prove the world wrong. Maybe I can dream.

'What about Denny?' I try and stop my lip quivering.

'He'll be here,' says Tiff. 'Just do him proud, kid.'

Kwaku pats me on the back. 'Knock her dead, Molly.'

My breath's heavy.

Three rounds.

A minute-and-a-half each.

That's all.

I hold up my hands in my gloves.
They feel solid,
like I could cause proper damage
    with them.
It's only four-and-a-half minutes
    tops.
I can do that.
Problem is,
if *my* hands are weapons,
·then hers on the other side of the door
    are weapons too. And unlike me,
        she'll know how to use them.

MOLLY 'T-REX' LEVINE VS JANET 'HAWK-EYE' HASSAN

PRE-BOUT

Rap music. Cheers. Eyes, eyes on me. The gacky smell of coffee. People shout. I don't care. I'm looking for Denny. Tears. Blurred eyes. I seriously don't want to fight without him.

'Go on,' says Frank. 'Get in there and show them what you're made of.'

I bend down. Put my foot on the canvas, chuck my towel over the ropes.

Tiff grits her teeth, almost growls. 'Go get 'em, girl.'

Janet stares across the canvas at me. She looks lethal. Her eyes like an animal's. I swing my head, side to side, warm up my muscles. See her shiny Nike trainers, so different from my grubby non-brand ones that are falling apart . . . No time for that now. My eyes lock with hers. She pushes her mouthguard in. Points. Thumps her chest. I know what that means. She wants to kill me.

Where the hell is Denny?

Ding ding ding!

ROUND 1

The crowd is blackness
my heart pounds
boom boom – boom boom
I'm all alone

just me and her
we dance – foot to foot
eyes locked together
she jabs . . . I go low

'Good, Molly!' Frank shouts.
I look round at him
she clips me on the chin –
ouch – idiot

I stumble – find my feet
Kwaku: 'Throw a punch, Molly!'
I move forward
swing my right . . . swing my left

my hips swing with my arms
she laughs – Tiff: 'Feet, Molly!'
Crack – lands in my head
she's too close

I recover – but
a solid shot *smack* in my ribs
sickness – in my gut
she picks up the pace

left jab – right hook
solid combinations
whack   whack   oof
Frank: 'Get back into it!'

She's all power
accuracy instinct
I defend – guard up
but it's no use –

endless rage
ding ding ding –
end of round one.

Two more rounds of this?
Pant, pant, pant.
Mate. I'm dead meat.

CORNER

[Water. Dry mouth. I gulp. Heavy breaths.]
Me: Where's Denny?
Frank: Never mind that. What're you doing out there? Get your head in the fight and Denny out of it.
Me: He said he'd be here. Why isn't he here?
Frank: *[mopping my head]* What did I just say? Head in the fight. She's wiping the floor with you.
[I swig again, shallow my breath.]
Frank: Focus. She's knackered with all those shots she's given you. Her range is too long – that's why you're missing her face. Work the body, get her on the ropes. You can claw this back, Molly.

Ding ding ding!

Me: *Damn you, Denny.*

ROUND 2

She lunges at me
I trip – my left foot
clips the back of my shin
the ropes catch me

thud thud thud
ah! I choke gobs of air
she's hungry
and I'm her meal

she lands a clean punch
whack
I go to the canvas
the lights above swirl

the crowd screams
I'm an idiot
Frank: 'Get up, Molly, get up!'
My legs are jelly

my cheeks burn
everyone is staring
I grip the ropes – stumble again
laughing laughing laughing

Kwaku: 'Come on, Molly!'
The ref's counting
the whole place
watches watches watches

shame fills me
I try again –
but there's nothing left
what a mess

all eyes on me –
ref counts down
what a bleedin' joke
I am . . .

she wins
it's over
and so am I.

POST-BOUT

I chuck my gloves at the bench, kick the locker.

Tiff pats my shoulder, a pitying look on her mug. 'Let it out, girl.'

I slam the locker with my hand. It clunks, rings harsh in my ears. Don't care. 'I hope karma chews him up and spits him out and makes him feel as stupid as I feel right now and . . .'

Kwaku comes in. 'You all right, mate?'

I'm too embarrassed to look at him.

Frank lets out a huge sigh. 'I told Denny you wasn't ready. He wouldn't have it. We'll sort you out. Next time, you'll destroy her.'

He has to be having a blimmin' laugh.

No way am I going to do that again.

CATERPILLAR

I can't get comfy in my bed. Nasty things that I want to say to Denny are doing my nut it. It feels like there are too many tabs open. Racing thoughts, one after the other, are screaming at me, making my blood boil.

You're selfish.
>*You're a bad brother.*
>>*I hate you.*
>>>*Don't talk to me.*

Nothing you can say will make it better.

He ain't home or replying to texts.

nothing.

I ain't gonna c-h-a-s-e him.
He can do one.

Idiot's probably waiting till I'm asleep
Z Z Z
before he comes home.

What a coward.
What a chicken.
I hate him.
I don't care if he never comes back again.

Every last bit of me *aches*. A huge bruise on my ribcage and shoulder is pure agony. My headache's evil too.

PAIN!

No one at home knows I've had a fight, obviously. I can't even get sympathy from Mum, or even a flippin' painkiller. Denny's good and proper screwed me over. Right on my tod I am.
Hurting.
Angry.

Creak, creak.
Click, click.
Thud, thud.
Snore, snore.

Every sound echoes.
Louder than a foghorn.
But – still – no – bleedin'
Denny.

Dad's in bed as usual. Mum's watching telly in the living room. Every little creak and crack puts me into fight mode. Denny can come back as late as he likes. I bet they won't treat me that well when I'm eighteen. It doesn't matter anyway – I'm going to wait up and go mental at him. I might have lost the fight, but I've still got a half-decent right hook and I ain't afraid to whack him right in his nut. Or worse. I tell you that for nothing.

Angry thoughts bubble . . . bleed through me. The night feels so so long.

Mum comes in. It's about half midnight. 'Baby, you dunno where Denny is, do you?'

'I don't give a monkey where he is. Could be in a ditch for all I care.' I can't even hide it from Mum.

'You two had a fight?' Mum sits on the bed, brushing my bruised ribs with her leg. She gives me a little grin, like she knows all my secrets.

I grunt in pain. Wonder if she knows about my fight. 'No, he's just a pain in the arse.'

Mum raises an eyebrow. 'Language.'

I grunt.

'You need some shut-eye by the looks of it.'

y	n
e	o
a	d
h	s

get some sleep
  You need it
  after today.

She winks, pulls the duvet up over me, tucks it in at the sides.

'There, like a caterpillar.' She leans down, kisses my head.

N I G H T Y N I G H T, M O L L Y D O L L Y

Part of me doesn't want her to leave. Part of me wants her to take my pain away with her. Like she did when I was little. If I ask her, I know she would. But these days it feels awkward. I ain't a baby anymore. So instead I say, 'Night, Mum.'

She leaves the door ajar, just enough to let the light in.

Old habits.

I wriggle down into my caterpillar. The anger about Denny and pain in my ribs fade, eyes soften.

I wake up. Look towards the door. Check my phone. 04.00.

Thudding.

BOW BELLS

I was up earlier than I was used to for a Saturday morning, waiting for my brother, Denny, outside Duke's boxing club.

He was late.

I looked the place up and down. It was nothing special. Just a worn-out building tucked away on Kempton estate.

Couldn't find it at first.

Didn't even have a sign.

I'd never been before. I was only allowed when Denny was fighting at the old man's club and that was different. Mum was with me then.

I squared up, made myself feel bigger, ignored the little voice inside my head saying I didn't belong there. Instead, I listened to the one in my heart, like Denny had taught me.

> *I want to be the best boxer in East London.*
> *It don't matter where I'm from, it's how hard I work.*
> *This is my dream and I'm going to rise.*

Some bloke, about Denny's age and as wide as a bus, marched out, a shabby boxing bag perched on his shoulder. He shoved it into an open van.

'You all right, love?' He dusted his hands off on his jeans.

'Yeah, just meeting someone.' I turned away quick before he tried to talk to me any more. *Denny must still be inside.* I shoved my head round the door. It was murky and stank of sweat. A massive mural of two fighters boxing covered the main wall. Next to it, a double door led to the gym, where the boxing ring took pride of place. Thuds, clunks and manly banter echoed through the walls.

I couldn't do it.

I turned to run out and

Smack
    – ouch! –
    a whack,
    right in my nut.

I scrunched my eyes up, rubbed my skull, twisted my face at the pain.
My eyes flickered open,
a tall kid with a
brushed-out afro
rubbed his head too.

    'Sorry, mate. Was rushing.
    I'm late. Him in there'll
    have my guts for garters
    if I'm not on time.'

The boy opened the door, waited for me to follow.
    'You coming in?'
A sunny smile lit his entire face,
like he was the happiest kid alive.

I suppose you would be,
if you could afford a pair
of Nike Airs, like the ones
he had on.
    All right for some, innit?

Feeling put on the spot,
I took the door.
    No excuses now.

Music blared,
the ground buzzed

    with the *crunch* –
    punch, swoosh –
    skip, rap –
    beat.

Happy Boy legged it down the hall towards the ring and disappeared round the corner. I took a massive breath and went in, trying to be brave, needing to find Denny.

It was packed full of blokes kitted out in expensive sports gear, some skipping, others thrashing punchbags. Some small and skinny. Others tall, with massive bulging muscles. They was all being shouted at by some old fella in a red cap. 'Focus. Footwork,' he was saying. 'Champions can do ten, Jago. How many have you got?'

Denny wasn't there.

I waited for someone to notice me. To chuck me out. Tell me I wasn't welcome. That the PE kit I had on was a joke. But no one looked up. Excitement and nerves fizzed in my belly. *Oh my God*, I was actually inside Duke's boxing club.

I moved further into the hall. Up close, the boxing ring was less epic. The canvas was scuffed and pure filth, the ropes shoddy and frayed. Over the other side of the room was an office with a glass window, looking in onto the hall.

Happy Boy sat on the floor, doing his laces. He looked up, gawped at me and waved. I pretended to gander one of the hundreds of posters of boxers plastered on the walls. All the greats – Ali, Eubank, The Packman. I knew most of them, even the ones in black and white, like Rocky Marciano. I'd watched them all on YouTube and dreamed of being like them a thousand times.

The *crunch*
> – punch, *swoosh*
> – skip, *rap*
> – swished all round me.

It was enough to make me dizzy.
> Muscles.

Packed into arms, chests, even legs.

'You Denny's?' a gruff voice echoed behind me.

I turned round. It was the old bloke with the red cap. He had a crabby face and gold rings on every finger, even his pinkie. *Is everyone round here rich or something?*

'Yeah, and I've got a name. It's Molly.' I stood myself tall, even though I didn't feel it inside.

He huffed, rolled his eyes in a proper exaggerated way. 'Right.'

He obviously didn't want me there, but he could've had manners about it.

'Name's Frank.' He wiped his hands on a grim-looking cloth.

'Frank Tessie?'

'Heard of me, have you?' His accent was one of the most hard-core cockney accents I'd heard in my lifelong life. He must have been proper old school East End.

'Sort of.' I bit my lip.

'Well, don't believe everything you're told.' He huffed again, his face like a twisted tree. 'Den's gonna be late. Let's grab you some gloves.'

'It's fine, I'll wait.' He obviously already knew I was poor and couldn't afford my own.

'I ain't got time to mess round. Let's get on with it.'

'Fine.'

Frank poked his head round the locker room door and waved me over. 'Safe to come in.'

It was even more rank than the gym, if that's possible. The light flickered and the locker doors hung off their hinges, but it was good to escape the noise.

Get away from all those muscles.

That weird smiley kid.

'Den's a great little fighter. Salt of the earth, that boy.'

I nodded, not knowing what to say.

'Great spirit too, but no restraint.' He rooted through a stack of grubby old gloves that were piled up on the floor. 'These'll have to do. They're probably a bit big, but they're the smallest I've got.'

He chucked a pair of manky black ones at me. They landed heavily in my belly, all soggy and stinking of stale sweat. 'These ain't red. Denny promised me red ones.'

Frank screwed up his mouth. 'This ain't a fashion parade. You get what you're given.'

Get what you're given.

The words echoed in my head.

Like skanky gloves are all I was worth.

The door flung open,
the *crunch* –
     punch,
swoosh – skip, *rap* –
beat, gushed back in.

'Ha,
see you've met old Frankie boy then?'
It was Denny.

I leaped across the room, wrapped my arms round him. 'Bout bleedin' time.' I let go. I was meant to be angry. I shoved him. 'You're late!'

'Woah! Easy, tiger.' Denny pulled me in and ruffled my hair.

'I'll leave yous to it. My office, Den, sharpish,' said Frank and off he toddled.

Denny pulled some baccy out of his pocket and rolled a fag.

I lobbed the gloves at him, embarrassed. 'These ain't red and they stink.'

Denny stuck his fag behind his ear. 'I'll sort it, kiddo. Soon as. I swear.'

I gave him my best snide look.

'Anyway, it ain't about the gloves, it's the boxer in them, ain't it?' He winked.

I tried not to smile, but it was impossible to stay mad at him.

He clapped his hands together. 'Right, let's get lively. You got training gear?'

'I've only got my PE kit.' It was getting too small for me, and I yearned for some proper boxing gear, but we couldn't even afford food half the time, let alone luxuries.

'That'll do for now. I'll get you some proper gear soon. Everlast, the whole shebang.'

I nodded, even though I knew it wasn't likely.

'Get changed. I'll see what Frank wants, then we'll wrap your hands. There's a proper knack to it.'

'In here?' I said, thinking about everyone in the gym.

'Course not. Frank said you can use the cupboard. It's out the corridor, on the left. Meet you in the sparring room in a sec.' He pointed at a dingy-looking door, then left.

OLD BILL

The thuds turn to voices.
Who's that at four a. m.?
I listen, still tucked up in bed.
Wipe sleep from my eyes.

'We're looking for Mr Dennis Levine,
in connection with a serious incident
at Duke's boxing club.'

'My card . . .
contact us . . .
if you hear anything . . .
It's in your best interests . . .
The truth always comes out . . .
This is a serious matter . . .'

'Right . . .
we'll be seeing you.
And remember –

   if

       you

          see

             him,

do the right thing.'

WHAT THE . . .?

I slip carefully into the front room.
Mum's sitting on the settee, smoking a fag.
Staring.
Like she ain't even there.
I don't know what to do.
So I sort of hover, feeling like a tool.

Thoughts buzz round me.
Denny wouldn't do that.
   . . . Would he?
Nah,
   he's a good guy.

But then, he did miss my fight.
And I had to admit,
   that was odd.

I tiptoe back to my room.

Break into Mr Weaver's internet,
cos we can't afford our own.

Send a bunch of WhatsApps,
my fingers sprinting
across my phone.

old bill's been round

come home

denny you bleeding moron. this
ain't funny no more

mums going spare

sry i was crappy before

let me know ur all right

Denny?

HELLO?

???????

Idiot

Maybe I should look up more about this blimmin' crime Denny's meant to have done. I'm so desperate. I type in the name of the bloke who was found beaten: *Harry Wi–*

Delete, delete, delete, delete, delete, delete . . . finger hovers . . . nah, delete.

I'm too scared about what I'm going to find.

I climb back into bed. Feel cold as hell, even though the heating is on full blast. Even the heaviness of my duvet doesn't take away this deep dark feeling inside my tummy. All I feel is empty.

'I'm sorry, Denny,' I say. Cos something in me makes me feel like all my anger made him go missing, made the Old Bill turn up. After all, I did say those nasty words about him. I did say, '*I don't care if he never comes back again.*'

I've got the day off school. Mum said it was better and, to be honest, it is, cos I don't wanna go anywhere in case Denny comes back. And God knows what people would be saying at school. I've spent all day checking my phone, rung him a thousand times. Every time I've looked at my messages, a spark of hope's bubbled in my belly, but I ain't even got a blue tick, never mind an answer.

Morning turns to day.

I overhear Dad crying
in the bathroom.
The sob sob sobbing
leaves a sick giddy feeling
all over me.

The police are back,
getting narky with Mum,
like she knows something
and is hiding Denny.

Even if she is,
      even if Denny's done in
      ten people . . .

Nobody round our way's a grass.

Especially not on your own family.
If things get tricky,
it's an unspoken law on the estates –
we sort it ourselves.
You don't tell Ol' Bill
nothing.

Ever.

Unless you want a good hiding.
In which case go ahead.
Your funeral.

Day turns to night.

I make Mum a cuppa.
Put it down in front of her.
She doesn't even look at me.

    'It's all right, Mum.
    He'll be home soon.
    I swear. I can feel it.'

Mum slides her hand across
the table, cups mine with it.
Squeezes.

    'It's getting late, Molly.
    Why don't you get to bed?'

I can't sit here a moment longer.
Doing nothing is doing my nut in.

My fingers tap, tap, tap his name.
Harry Wilson, Duke's gym.

I click on the first link.
A news article.

ine
re

Man found battered outside East London gym

Members of an East London gym, Duke's, were shocked last night to find Harry Wilson, 21, of East Ham, lying badly beaten in an alleyway at the back of the famous gym.

Detective Inspector Oyoye of the Metropolitan Police said, "Mr Wilson was heavily bruised and has sustained serious head injuries and multiple fractures. He is currently receiving treatment in hospital where he remains in an induced coma in ICU. This attack was brutal and unsophisticated in nature and we are currently wanting to talk to a Mr Dennis Levine in connection with this crime."

DI Oyoye went on to say that members of the public should not approach Mr Levine as he could be dangerous.

Police would like anyone who has any information regarding this crime to contact them on

I stop reading.
Scroll back up.

Unsophisticated in nature.

And that's when I know for a fact –
beyond just my gut –
    Denny did not do this.

He's a trained boxer.
If he wanted to hurt someone,
I can promise you for nothing –
    it would *not* be unsophisticated.

WAITING

I wait.

Wait for Denny to answer.

Wait. Wait. Wait. Wait. Wait. Wait. Wait. Wait. Wait. Wait. Wait.

Wait – tick, wait – tock. Wait – tick, wait – tock. Wait – tick, wait – tock.

Waiting is nothing but time chucked away.

Click refresh.

Click refresh.

I wait.

I wait.

I wait.

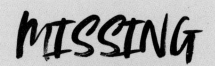

**DENNY LEVINE
18 YEAR OLD. MALE.
LAST SEEN 20TH OCTOBER.
5 FT 11 INCHES.
DARK HAIR.**

POSTERS

We're handing out posters.

I dream.

Imagine
Denny reading one
and laughing at us
for overreacting.

Then

coming   right   through   the   door.

His cheeky grin.

Dimples,
like Granddad's.

Saying,
      'Put the kettle on, Molls,
      I'm parched.'

But he doesn't
and he isn't.
Or he won't.
Or can't?

I dunno.
It's too confusing.

And now
I'm getting
proper
scared.

MISSING

Denny's been gone a week now and I dunno what the hell to do about it. We aren't allowed to report him missing cos he's a wanted man and the Old Bill reckon he's on the run. But how can a man who's innocent be on the run? I'll tell you how – they're forcing him on the run, cos they've *accused him of doing shit he ain't bleedin' done, that's why*. Flippin' joke it is. Morons the lot of them. They don't know him like I do.

Dad and his mate have been searching every day from wake till sleep. Dad looks a state. I don't think he's stopped to eat. All he keeps saying is he wants his boy back. He's trying so hard to look after Mum too. He ain't gone to hide under his duvet cover, not once. It's the longest I've seen him out of bed for months. It's like he's got purpose for the first time in his life. Funny how something bad happening can give a man motivation.

I beg Dad to let me help find Denny.

'No, Molly Dolly.' He puts his arms right around me, squeezes me in close, whispers gently in my ear, his voice cracking, 'I need you to stay here, look after Mum. She needs you right now. Can you do that?'

His affection makes me squirm and I'm annoyed at feeling like a spare part, but he's right. Mum needs me. 'Course, Dad,' I say.

I can't stop imagining the world with Denny cut out of it, cos there are spaces everywhere I go . . .

A space on the chair he sits at for brekkie,
a space where he sleeps,
a space on the coat rail
where his Fred Perry always hangs.

I squint my eyes,
try to imagine him in his usual spaces.
As if my imagining him will bring him back.
But it's no use.
The more I look,
the less he's there.
He's gone, and there's
nothing
I can do about it.

NOSY BUGGER

It's Sunday and I ain't been in school all week, but Dad says I've got to go tomorrow, so I'm getting my stuff together. I grab my pencil case from the windowsill and check for Denny out the window for the hundredth time this morning.

I have to double-take.

Kwaku's sitting on the bench across from the common.

What's he doing there?

I chuck my trainers and hoodie on. 'Just going out,' I shout down the hallway at Mum. Wait for a reply, but nothing. Slam the door as hard as I can.

She can't ignore that.

'What the hell're you doing here?'

'Molly, thank God.' Kwaku jumps up from the bench. 'Are you all right? I was wondering why you wasn't in practice. Frank told me what happened.'

'If you've come to have a nosy, don't bother, there's nothing to see.'

Kwaku looks upset. 'Nosy? No. I was worried. I know how tight you and Denny are.'

'What you doing out here then? Why not knock for me?'

'I've never been to your flat, remember? I thought I'd chance running into you on the estate.'

I soften a bit. 'Well, that's dumb.'

'Yeah, maybe.' He rubs the back of his head, his trademark village-idiot look plastered on his mug.

I want to be angry, but I ain't got the strength and, if I'm being honest, I fancy the company right now.

I sit on the bench, pick a flat stone up off the ground, scrape it on the bench, needing to give my hands something to concentrate on. 'I dunno what I'm gonna do,' I say.

Kwaku sits next to me, says nothing back.

Denny always says that silence means more to people than words. Sometimes, when your world is falling apart, it's nice that someone just wants to listen, instead of yapping at you, trying to fill your head with their own opinions and stuff.

Gary from the top floor walks past. I pretend not to see him – can't stand the thought of having to answer questions. I scratch lines into the bench with the stone. It looks how I imagine my heart looks.

Splintered.

'Are you gonna come back to Duke's?'

I dust the splinters off the bench, start scratching again, dig deeper into the wood like I want to hurt it. 'Joking, ain't you? Not with all this going on – and not after losing my fight too. I've got some dignity.'

Kwaku looks like he's wrestling with something in his head. 'When I'm stressed, the gym kind of helps. Like with the anger. It takes my mind off things.'

'I don't want to take my mind off things. I want to be sad.'

'Fair enough.' He slouches further into the bench.

I feel bad. 'Sorry about your dad,' I say. 'What happened?'

Kwaku shrugs, ignores the question. 'So, you've got no idea where Denny is?'

'If I had an idea, do you think I'd be sitting here with your dumb face?'

He got out some gum, gave me one. 'My mum said people go missing all the time then show up.'

'Well, my dad said that after the first three days you're most likely dead and no one is ever gonna see you again.' Tears sting my eyes. I put them back before I make an idiot of myself.

Kwaku pats my knee. His touch is awkward, but sort of nice. Not in a fancying way though. It ain't like that.

'I'm here for you. I know we haven't known each other long or . . . whatever—' He stops and tuts. 'What I'm trying to say is, I got your back.' He puts out his hand, offers a fist for a bump.

I knock his hand lightly. 'Thanks.'

It goes quiet again,

but this time the wrong kind of quiet.

The thoughts come back.

Anger.

Questions.

Bubbling, bubbling.

Fists tight.

Jaw tight.

Shoulders too.

So much buzzing

    round my head.

Buzz. Buzz. Buzz.

They creep down my neck,
crawl right inside my chest,
like hands clawing my insides,
trying to reach right out from my belly.

Silent screaming.

'I don't get it,' I blurt.

'What?' Kwaku bounces up from his slump.

'Denny can't have hurt that bloke. He ain't violent. He ain't nasty. If only that Harry bloke would wake up out of his coma, he could tell them. Tell them who it really was. Denny's decent. Yeah, he boxes, but boxing's not violent. Denny says boxing is discipline, says mindless violence is a joke. He ain't "unsophisticated" like they said. Idiots. And, he wouldn't leave me. Something bad's happened and he can't get back or he's . . .' I choke. 'He's . . .'

Kwaku catches my words. 'It's OK, Molly.'

He rubs my arm. I let myself rest my head on his shoulder. The tightness sinks out of me and into him. My breath comes back a bit.

'You should look for him,' he says.

I lift my head back up from his shoulder.

'If the Ol' Bill can't find him, what makes you think I can?'

'Yeah, but feds dunno him like you do. Nobody does, and it sounds like you've already been doing your research on the internet.'

Kwaku's right. If anyone knows Denny, it's me. But then . . . 'If I knew him so well, I'd have worked out where he is already. . There's no point. It's impossible.'

'Nah, mate. Like Muhammad Ali said, "Impossible is nothing."'

'What does that even mean?'

'I know it's dark right now, Molly, but that's where you come in. Shine a light and you'll find Denny, I'm sure of it.'

It sounds great. But I can't face doing it alone. I take a deep breath and say it quickly, before I change my mind. 'Will you help me?'

He nods like a right blend.

'Damn straight I'm helping you. But only if you come back to the gym and train again. Don't throw it away – Denny wouldn't want that.'

I do miss Duke's. It's the only place left where I still feel I belong.

'You've got yourself a deal,' I say.

'Wicked! Man's always fancied being a detective. Anyway, you need someone to do the interview questions. I dunno if you've noticed, but you're not very good at being polite.' He lets his head fall to his knees, giggles like a freak.

I nudge him and put the stone in my pocket. 'Polite is overrated –' and for first time since Denny's gone missing, I let myself smile.

I let the light in.

WRAPS

I shuffled into
the cupboard
to change.

It was rammed
full of mops,
buckets, rubbish, brooms.

What a joke.
I barely fit in.
There's no light.
I hid under
my school shirt,
just in case someone
came in.
Listened hard
for footsteps.

Crunch – punch, *swoosh* – skip, *rap* – beat.

Darkness.
Smallness.
Everywhere.

I pulled my long mousy
hair into a pony,
kicked the door open,
wandered to the sparring room,
sat on the shoddy
wooden bench against
the wall.
Picked
the paint
with my thumb.
Tried to avoid looking at

myself
in the mirror.

I couldn't resist.

There I was.

Short.

Floppy.

Bumpy chest.

Lank greasy hair.

Cute freckles.

Non-brand

knock-off

sports gear.

Yuck.

Not

a muscle

in sight.

I couldn't knock a fly out,

let alone an actual person.

The door flung open, melting my thoughts away. 'Come on, let's wrap those hands.'

Denny went to his locker. It had his name on – *Dino Den* – that Grand-dad had called him when he was alive, before I was born. He grabbed a bundle of yellow bandages and turned back to me. 'You know why boxers wrap their hands?'

'So it don't hurt punching?'

'Nah, that's what people think. But it's science. Boxing's a blood sport, Molly –' he put his fists up – 'and your mitts are your weapons.'

I looked at my hands. They were small and ordinary, the absolute opposite of weapons.

'The wraps fasten your joints together.'

'What? My hands will break if I don't wrap them?'

Denny laughed. 'Not exactly. The wraps tighten a solid fist.'

I hated being wrong.

I wanted to impress.

'See, if you wrap up well, you're less likely to get hurt.' He held the wrap out in front of me.

I held my hand out.

'There's a proper way to do it. I'll always help you, cos doing it yourself's hard.' Denny made a loop and hooked it over my thumb. I gave him my full attention, to show I meant business. 'Always wrap behind the hand, like this.' He pulled the wrap round underneath my knuckles.

'Does it have to go that way?'

Denny's dimples dented his cheeks. 'Yeah, you've got to go round the back of the hand so the wrap tightens when you make a fist.' He pulled it round my wrist. Wrapped it one, two, three times. 'Watching?'

I nodded.

'Good. So now you want to pull it over your thumb and make three X shapes, starting with the pinkie, then you do the other fingers.'

My hand started to feel stiff.

'Now you lock the thumb. This time, you want to go over the palm, wrap the knuckles three times and – last – over the wrist.' He rolled it round quick, squashed all the creases. When he'd finished, the wrap was dangling off my arm.

'Little hands.' He grinned. 'Like a T-Rex.' He wrapped it round a few more times then stuck it with Velcro, then pushed the manky old gloves on over the wrapping. 'There, how does it feel?'

I held my hand up and tested it.

Crunch

It felt snug.

Swoosh

I tightened my fingers.

Rap rap rap

My fist felt safe.

I felt safe.

It was like being held together . . .

and my heart
    drummed
    as I imagined
    landing
    my very first
    punch.

DENNY'S ROOM

Mum's still sitting where I left her, at the kitchen table, smoking another fag.

Moving to the sink, I grab myself a glass of water. 'Any news?'

She shakes her head.

I wait for her to say something. Anything. But she just sits there staring at the window. There's no point hanging about, so I head to my room, leave her to it.

Denny's bedroom door's ajar. The smell of Lynx deodorant wafts out from inside.

Is he home?

Has he snuck in?

I creep in, expect to see him sitting on his bed, like he always is, on his laptop messaging mates or whatever bird he has on the go.

A fag hanging from his mouth.

That cheeky, dimpled smile of his.

But the room is still empty

empty

empty.

I brush my hand over his West Ham duvet. It looks like Mum's made his bed. Fresh sheets and everything. She probably wanted it special for when he gets back.

I take a gander at his desk. Brush things aside. Hoping for a clue. Hoping for anything. It's messy. Old boxing mags, an ashtray still full. An unopened can of Sprite.

His favourite.

I sit on his bed, breathe him in, try to feel close to him.

My foot catches on something under the bed. I tip my head upside down, peer underneath. My hair swings from side to side.

I gander his Fred Perry jacket.
But that can't be right.
Denny goes nowhere
without his Fred Perry.

I yank it out.

Rummage
through the pockets.

What the . . . ?

    A phone.
    His phone.
    Denny's blinkin' phone!
It's been here
the whole time.

Oh my God!
It might have something
on it!

But hang on –
why is it even here?

Denny only leaves it at home
    when he goes running.
Did he go
running the morning
of my fight and
    something happen?

I make a mental note.

I try to switch it on.
It's out of battery.
I shove it in my hoodie, safe,
then check the other pocket.

His boxing notepad.
Routines, fight tactics
sprawled across the pages.
Nothing of interest.

    'What're you doing in here?'

Mum!
I jump so hard
I almost hit the ceiling.

'Sorry, Mum. I was just . . .'

Her eyes are dead.
It isn't worth arguing.

She sits on the bed,
pulls Denny's old
Flumpy bear close to her,
up to her chest.
'I wasn't trying to upset you.
I miss him too, you know.'

BlankSilenceInReturn

Anger bubbles.

I leave her there to rot
in her own misery.

Head to my room.

I need to check Denny's phone.

CHARGING . . .

I plug it to charge.
    Straightaway.
The battery icon fills –

– so – – slow – – – it – – –
                        hurts.

My heart is motionless.

    Argh!

    Hurry up!

The screen finally flicks on.

    Three
    Stupid
    Words

PLEASE ENTER PIN

STAND **heavy**
    on the screen.

SOMETHING TO HANG OUR HAT ON

Kwaku's late.

We're meant to be meeting outside Vic's Minimart, on my estate, at 7 a.m., but it's quarter past and no sign of him. I lean against the wall, tuck my nose under the rim of my hoodie, puff out hot air to warm my face. The bricks are icy on my back. I shove forward, scuff my feet.

Anything to get warm.

George's is unnerving in the early morning light. More and more, since Denny's gone, everything has looked that way. Like secrets are lurking round every corner.

'Hey, sorry I'm late.' Kwaku's voice comes from behind me.

I turn round. The blend is wearing shorts. 'Bout bloomin' time!' I puff a cloud of cotton wool air in his face.

He chucks his bag at the ground. 'Yeah, sorry. My mum was suspicious about me being up early.' He rubs his hands together, kicks his bag against the shop wall and sits on it. 'Brrr, cold innit?'

'You know you're wearing shorts, right? It ain't exactly sunbathing weather.'

'Got PE first lesson. Anyway, what you found? The suspense is killing me.'

I shove Denny's phone at him and sit down beside him on the ground.

'It's an old iPhone . . .' He looks at me, twists his lips in confusion.

I nod. 'Just cos it's old, don't mean it don't work. Can't all be fancy like you!'

'Sorry. I didn't mean . . .' He huffs. 'Why you showing me it?'

'Thought you was meant to be brainy. It's Denny's, ain't it.'

His eyes almost fall out of his head. 'No freaking way! How'd you find this?'

'It was under his flippin' bed the whole time. I dunno . . . makes me think he left in a hurry – or went out for a run and something happened.'

'Sounds a bit suss? Maybe it's a clue?' He switches it on, it buzzes a welcome tone, the screen's light flickers in his eyes. 'Have you tried the normal ones?'

'What's the normal ones?'

'I dunno, like, 1234?'

'Course I have. I ain't that thick.'

'1111?'

I huff. 'Yes.'

'Denny's birthday?'

He's annoying me. 'Yes. That too!'

'What about your birthday?'

'Bleedin' heck! Why would it be *my* birthday?'

'Um, cos Denny thinks you're a legend. You're the apple of his eye. Duh.'

I shake my head. 'Don't be a melon.' I pull my arms round myself, not cos I'm cold this time.

'Try it – nothing to lose.' He shoves it in my hand. 'Go on.'

'Yes, there is. Something to lose, that is. I've already tried eight codes, and after ten the phone gets wiped. It's some security thing.'

'So, you've got two more goes. You've got to try it.'

He's right. I have to try it.

Denny's phone could be the key

to sorting this stupid mess.

I turn it back on.

Punch my birthday in.

Hold my breath.

Again, those five horrible words plaster the screen . . .

WRONG PASSCODE
1 ATTEMPT LEFT

I whack the phone with the palm of my hand. 'See! Now I've only got one try left.' My belly feels wobbly.

'Careful, you'll break it. Did you find anything else?'

'Just his boxing notebook, with all his workouts in it.' I pull it out from my back pocket and gave it to him.

He sifts through it.

'There's nothing to look at,' I say. 'They're just useless bits of paper. I dunno why I'm even carrying it round with me.' It's a lie. I know why. Denny used to carry the notepad everywhere. Having it on me makes me feel like he's still with me.

He skims through the notes, training schedules, dates for fights, like it's some classic book written by some ancient, boring writer. Then he stops turning the pages, holds the pad to my face. 'Woah. Told you Denny thinks you're a legend.'

I push the notepad back away. 'I never said he didn't, did I?'

'Man's gotta love you if he spends that much on your gloves.'

'Nah, he's skint. Probably got them off the back of a lorry and got them stitched down the market.'

'No. Look.' He shoves a receipt in my face again.

I grab it off him.

```
        RECEIPT OF SALE

   _ _ _ _ _ _ _ _ _ _ _ _


   RED GLOVES
   PLUS
   STITCHING - GOLD
   'T-REX'

   £300
```

'Nah.' I shake my head.

'What?'

'Nah. No way. Denny's not got that kind of cash. Something ain't right.'

'Is there an address on it?'

I look.

```
   _ _ _ _ _ _ _ _ _ _ _ _


   BAINS' SPORTS EMPORIUM,
       PLACHETT ROAD
```

Kwaku does a weird sitting–down dance. His spongy hair sways on his head.

'Enough dancing!' I dunno how he has this much energy in the morning. I get up, grab my bag. 'Come on, we've got to go. Now. See if anyone remembers Denny. This don't feel right. Maybe it's connected somehow.'

Kwaku ganders his phone. 'Good idea, but we can't go now – we'll be late for school.'

I don't want to wait. 'Forget school, let's go.'

'We can't. We've got to keep it low key. We don't want anyone asking what we're up to, do we?'

'True.' I hate it, but he's right.

He grabs his bag off the ground, walks away backwards. 'Meet down by the station, before gym?'

'Fine, whatever.'

'See ya later, when your legs are straighter!' He sticks his tongue out and sprints off.

It's going to be a long day.

Denny was waiting at the gates after school.

'What you doing here?'

He zipped up his Fred Perry jacket, right to the top. 'Waiting for you. *Brrr*, it's blimmin' taters out here.'

'That's what you get when you wear a little jacket in winter. What's up?'

Denny slapped his hands together, cupped them over his mouth, blew his breath into them. 'Got something for you, ain't I? Come on, it's at Duke's.'

'I ain't training tonight, Den. I done six miles this morning – I'm crackered. Anyway, I'm meeting Kwaku.'

Denny raised an eyebrow. 'Kwaku, eh?'

I tutted, walking away. 'It ain't like that. Boys are gross and, to be honest, pretty flipping dumb.' Denny raced after me.

'Probably best. I ain't ready to beat up boys who break your heart yet.'

I gave him a funny look. 'If I get a boyfriend, it'll be me breaking hearts and I won't need you fighting my battles. Gonna be British champ, ain't I?' I squeezed the non-existent muscle in my arm.

Denny rolled a fag. Cloudy puffs of air blew from his lips as he sealed it with his tongue. 'You know you actually need to train to become a champ, right? Not be a lazy mare, like you are?'

'Haha, very funny.'

'Anyway, you coming with, or what? No training. Swear.' He stuck his fag behind his ear, put his hands up in the air to prove he wasn't crossing his fingers.

I flicked him right in the nose. 'Fine, you daft git. But it better be quick.' Duke's was dead. All echoey, like an abandoned warehouse. It was weird seeing it empty, no people, no noise. Sort of creepy even. Like ghosts were hiding in the corners. No way I'd want to be in there on my tod.

'Frank ain't here then?' I looked at the office window, the lights were off. 'I thought he lived here.'

'He does, pretty much. But he's gone to see a man about a dog.' He tapped his nose, winked. 'Wait here.'

I sat on the edge of the ring, let my feet swing from side to side, while Denny went into Frank's office.

'Sorry, I never had no wrapping paper.' He came out holding his jacket, there was something under it. He held it out to me. 'Go on . . .' He looked stupidly excited.

I yanked the coat off.
Under it
were a pair
of red
shiny
gloves.

I grabbed them.

   'They're bloomin' lovely, Den!'
I couldn't believe it.
   No more sweaty,
   yucky,
   rank ones
      from the odds and ends box.
        No more,
           Looking like a poor, dirty scab.

'But how did you afford . . . ?'

'Never mind that, try them on.'

I didn't waste any time.
I shoved the left one on, then the right.
They were epic.

   'Stick them up then –
   I want a photo.'

I did my best boxer's pose,
saw the cuffs had gold letters,
turned my wrists to get a better look.

On my left glove . . .

                    T
                    on the right . . .
                            REX
          'T-Rex,' I whispered.
                    'Cor,
          these must've cost you a bomb.'
He smiled.
          'Don't worry about that.
          Only the best for you, kiddo.
          I knew the first time I wrapped your little hands
          You was a Tyrannosaur.'

          'But you're Dino Den . . .
          people might think I'm copying.'

Denny's dimples grew.
          'Molly "T-Rex" Levine,
          a family connection.
          Like Granddad named me.
          He helped me believe
          anything's possible.
          I wish you could have
          known him, Molls.'

          'Me too.'

          'Maybe we can make it a tradition.
          Like when we have kids and stuff.'
          'T-Rex does sound nifty.'
I leaped at him.
          'Thanks, Den.'

          'Woah! Easy, tiger –
          been working on that lunge,
          have you?'
He cuddled me back.
          He was the best brother
          in the world.

BAINS' SPORTS EMPORIUM

The shop's round the back of the train station, on an old industrial site. It's a lifeless, dusty place. Everything that used to be white has faded to a dingy beige. Piles of rubble, old tyres and bits of pipe dumped any old how. And it stinks of diesel.

'You sure this is right?' I ask Kwaku.

'Yeah, it's over here.' He moves ahead, forces me to rush after him.

Kwaku stops. 'This is it.'

It looks like a warehouse. All windows for walls, covered in massive red-and-white '50% OFF!' and 'WOW!!!' signs.

'Come on, let's get in there.'

There aren't any customers inside. It's dead, not even any music playing. The stench of plastic fills the air. The space is so wide, the ceilings so high, it feels empty, even though it's rammed with stuff. Not just boxing gear neither – there's stuff for every sport you can imagine, even ice hockey, and God knows who was playing that round our way. It might be cold in December, but that's just taking the piss. We go to the counter at the far end of the shop where a skinny dark-haired woman is sitting staring at a computer. She doesn't look up.

'Good afternoon, young lady –' Kwaku waves his hand in front of the woman's face. 'We wondered if you could answer a few questions?' He talks all posh, like Mum does when she's on the phone to the council begging for another budget loan.

The woman ain't in any hurry.

She presses her mouse,

    click click click,

        reorganises some papers, slides her greasy fringe off her face.

Kwaku looks at me like he has no idea what to do.

I slam my hand down on the counter. 'Oi! Do you work here or what, mate?'

She doesn't even flinch. 'If you need anything to do with sports gear, I'm your girl,' she says, not even looking up from her screen.

I ain't having this neek mug me off. I dig into my pocket, pull out the receipt, put it down in front of her.

'Do you remember the bloke who bought these?'

She stops

    tap tap tapping,

        but still doesn't look at us.

'We have an awful lot of customers. I dunno how you expect me to re-member. Anyway, I'm not the only one who works here. Might be Steve was working that day. Or Donna. Could have been Donna. Was it a Saturday?'

'Maybe if you had a proper look you'd remember.' I flatten out the receipt, point, give her my best evil face. 'He bought boxing gloves. Had a nickname stitched on them. T-Rex. See?' I shove the receipt closer, wanting to ram it in her face.

She huffs, pushes herself back on her stupid swivel chair, picks up the receipt, studies it a few seconds, then nods and chucks it back at the counter, like it isn't precious evidence.

'Yep.'

Kwaku looks at me again. 'Yeah what?'

She

    tap tap taps

        again. 'I remember the guy. Had money to burn, told me he wanted the most expensive gloves with the most expensive stitching. Fancied himself a bit of a wide boy.'

It doesn't sound like Denny at all. 'You sure?'

'Yeah, I am. Lad in a blue Fred Perry jacket, dark hair, late teens maybe.'

'Did you do the stitching?' asks Kwaku.

'You've got to be joking! That kind of thing needs a real expert. He came back to collect them.' She looks at her watch and rearranges the counter. She's got to be the most unhelpful woman on the planet. This is pointless . . .

'Anything else you can think of?' Kwaku pushes.

The shop assistant looks up at us for the first time. 'What is this about? I don't think I should be giving away so much information about our customers.'

'Never mind. Come on, Kwaku, this is a waste of bleedin' time.'

But Kwaku ain't giving up. 'It's her brother. He's missing. We won't say anything to get you in trouble, we just need some help.'

Her eyes soften.

She is human!

'Sorry, I honestly don't know nothing.'

'Come on, Kwaku, let's go.' I grab the receipt, storm away. Kwaku runs after me.

The

> click click click, tap tap tapping
> echoes, like our footsteps.

We make our way back out into the dingy yard, then further into town to get a bus to Duke's.

'It just don't ring true. Denny ain't no . . . what did she call him?'

'Wide boy. Kinda like a show-off.'

'I know what it means. I ain't thick.'

We sit down at the bus stop. I check my phone.

Nothing.

'Maybe he was excited cos he was getting you such an ace pressie.'

'Yeah. But that still doesn't explain where he got the money.'

'Savings?'

'Where from? Den didn't even have a job. Unless someone was paying him to do something dodgy. But I can't see him doing that neither.'

Our bus pulls up. I get my Oyster card out of my pocket. The receipt for Bains' Sports Emporium comes with it. I stare at it.

Three hundred pounds.

What did Denny have to do to get it? He isn't working, doesn't get paid, so it has to be something dodgy. But what?

'You getting on or what?' says Kwaku.

I nod, step into the bus.

A VIEW FROM THE CORNER

Skip, hop, skip
Denny, where are you?
Skip, hop, skip

Thud, duck, punch
Why were you being so cocky?
Thud, duck, punch

Barum barum, rap a beat
What's his password?
Barum barum, rap a beat

Molly jab, Molly dive
Where did you get the money?
Molly jab, molly dive

Ding goes the bell, spar spar
Where is he? Where is he?
Denny, Denny,
why did you leave me?
Ding goes the bell, spar spar

D   E   NNNNNNNNNNN   Y

On my way out the gym,
I run into Frank.
He's saying something to me,
but I can't hear over the

    thump, whack, whack, whack

of punches being landed,

the constant

clang, clang, clang

of the chains that hang
the punchbags, the
        hip hop

beats blasting from the stereo.

I cup my ear.

    'You what?'
I reply.
Practically shout.

    'You got a minute?'

    'I'm kind of in a rush.
    Wanna get home
    before it gets dark.'

He holds a hand to his mouth
to amplify his voice over the racket.
        'It won't take long.
        Let's get out of this noise.'

RANK

Frank's office is a blinkin' state. It stinks of stale fags and old-man deodorant. There are papers everywhere, even on the floor. Bits of hand tape stuck on his desk, empty tea cups with green growing in them.

The walls are a different story. Medals on shelves, pictures of him with boxers, a few belts. The usual boxing quotes.

'Sit down, I'll grab you a drink.'

I sit on a leather spinny chair. It's taped down the side with grey electrical tape. 'You need a trip to Ikea, Frank. This place is a mess.'

'No need. It's only me who comes in here most of the time. I like to call it "lived in".' He shoves a can of cola in front of me and a cuppa for him, then sits down on his side of the desk.

'Fair enough.' I rub my arms to warm them. It's blimmin' taters – he could've put the heating on. Such a tightwad. I zip up my hoodie.

'I'm glad you've come back to Duke's. I don't reckon Denny will forgive me if I don't watch out for you, while he's gone.'

'I don't need looking after.' I sip the cola It's as weak as gnats' pee, some fake supermarket brand.

He pulls his cap off, ruffles his white hair, puts his cap back on. 'Sure you don't. I was thinking . . . a lot of these youngsters, they come in here to keep out of trouble. It gives them a focus, what they don't get nowhere else.'

'Lucky them. Can we get this over with? I'm freezing and it's getting dark.' I shove the can on the desk, make a scrunched-up face.

'It's just . . . I was thinking, since you came back and Denny's not about – I ain't saying he won't come back, but while he's not, I mean – if you want . . . I'd be happy to train you. You're gonna need a coach. Your footwork's all out and we've got to do something about your defence.'

'Ain't a coach meant to give their fighters confidence?'

Frank smiles, deep cracks shadow his face. 'Hey, I didn't promise to give you an ego. But I can promise to get you on form. Get you another fight.'

I pull my hair up into a pony to keep my hands busy.

'You have a little think about it. Denny's like a son to me – no offence to your dad or nothing.'

'Everything's useless without him.' The words vomit from me.

'Tell me about it.' Frank fiddles with the gold rings on his slug-like fingers.

'Ain't you got no family?' I know nothing about Frank, apart from what Denny and Kwaku have said, which ain't much.

He dips his head, doesn't reply, his hands clasped against his mouth like he's trying to keep his words locked in.

'I had a son . . . He died.'

'I'm sorry.' I put my hands under my thighs, fidgeting in my seat. I don't know what else to say.

'It's all right. I've got this place, ain't I? That's why I get so attached to my fighters. Duke's is family now.'

I feel sorry for him and, deep down, I know I need the help. I want to fight. Want somewhere to go to escape reality. When I'm boxing, I ain't just some girl off the estates, or someone whose brother's wanted by the police 'All right then,' I say.

'All right what?'

'You can coach me. I only came back cos Kwaku made me promise, but if I'm gonna come, I might as well get good.'

'What's it to Kwaku?'

I pause, then decide. If Denny can trust Frank, so can I.

'Kwaku and me, we've got a deal. He helps me find Denny, I keep boxing.'

Frank holds his cuppa right tight to his chest. 'Molly, it's probably best you leave that to the grown-ups, love.'

'I've gotta try. I can't just sit around twiddling my thumbs like a plank.'

Frank looks like he's thinking. 'That Kwaku's a good lad.'

'Yeah. I didn't know posh people could be nice.'

'Ha! Kwaku ain't posh.'

'Compared to me he is. He's minted.'

'Life ain't always about money, Molly. It's about opportunity, and having the brains to spot it when it comes along and the guts to grab it with all your strength.'

'If you say so.'

Frank chuckles, shakes his head, sits forward, a look of concern on his face. 'So, what are these clues you've gone and found?'

I shrug, wonder if I've said too much. 'Nothing really. Just a receipt for the gloves he bought me. They was proper expensive – I dunno how he had the cash. So we went down the shop he bought them from, but it was a dead end. You don't know if Denny had a job or anything, do you?' I ask, realising this is an opportunity to find the answer to one bit of the puzzle.

Frank swirls his mug of tea. 'Not that I know of, no.'

'Oh.' Another dead end.

Suddenly Frank claps his hands loud. 'Righto. Enough of this moping round – we've got training to do.'

'I just finished, Frank.'

He spits out a proper belly chuckle. 'Ha! You're having a tinny, ain't you? That was just a warm-up.'

SEFFI

It's raining, which is bugging,
cos it's smudging my phone screen.
I'm scrolling through Denny's
friends on Facebook,
trying to think of mates
I can message and interrogate.

I stop dead at a photo of a girl,
perched flirty on some bloke's lap.
Her name's Seffi Evans.
It's a name that doesn't ring a bell.

But I zoom in anyway.
Call it gut instinct.
It's some goth-looking girl and
the lap she's sitting on
is his.

Denny's.

NOISE

Back out in the gym the noise of the music,
the *smack whack crack* of people punching bags
    was deafening.
I focused on Denny
followed him to the boxing ring.
    'Who's this little lady then, Den?'
It's another girl,
a woman!

'This is Molly, my little sister. Remember I told you about her?'
Denny wrapped his arm round me, bashing me up against him, squashing
my cheek.
    I shoved him away. 'Get off me, you melt.'
    'Name's Tiff. Pleased to meet you, love.' She patted my arm, firm, strong.
My eyes glazed with stars. She was amazing.
    She winked at Denny and headed for some weights that were all stacked
up in neat piles, each one bigger than the next.
    'You sure you don't want someone else training you?' Tiff heaved
a huge weight up to her chin like it was as light as a pen. 'Old Denny
boy here dunno much. He's more of a girl than both of us put together,'
she joked.

The *clank clank clank* of the weights.
One guy, about the size of a small car, lifted a huge weight,
his muscles flexed as though he was half man, half machine.
He grunted as he dropped it to the ground.

And he's just one of them.
Apart from Tiff,
and even she's built
like a brick shithouse.
    Muscles.
    Everywhere.
Her happy wide shoulders.

Her confident bulging biceps.

Her, successful, as if she ain't from where I'm from.

Happy in her own skin.

Tiny. **Me.**

Skint. **Me.**

No wins under my belt. **Me.**

And Tiff, a perfect specimen.

I'd never be like her.

Dizzy, dizzy, dizzy.

I can't handle it.

'Nah.' I turned back toward the changing room. 'This was a stupid idea. Dad was right. I don't belong here.'

Denny whipped quickly in front of me, grabbed my shoulders, turned me back round. 'Oh no you don't.'

I shoved him off. 'Everyone's gonna look at me. I feel like a right plum.'

'Who's looking at you? They ain't got time to look at you – they're too busy doing their own thing.'

I looked round the room. 'Is Tiff the only girl that comes here?'

'There's a girls' class up Bethnal Green, but it's not proper. This is the sort of club you come to if you want to compete. You want to compete, don't you?'

I looked at the taped-up punchbag next to us. 'It's still a dive.'

Happy Boy came out of the changing room, got in the ring with Frank and started bouncing about, his arms and legs lank and weedy.

'Who's that?'

Denny looked over. 'That's Kwaku. Defensively, he's a right nightmare, but he's got a bit of rhythm about him.'

I looked at him, all arms and legs. All named brands. Hair styled like some yuppy. Life was obviously treating him well. Bet he didn't have a care in the world.

HAPPY BOY

After training, it was spitting with rain. The cold damp relieved my clammy skin. There was no doubt about it, I was done in. Every inch of me was killing, from my calves up to my neck. I swear, even my lips hurt.

'Can you get home all right?' Denny zipped up his navy Fred Perry jacket, flicked his fingers through his dark shiny hair.

'You ain't coming with?'

He shifted from one foot to the other, buried his hands deep in his pockets. On the defence. 'Got a few errands to run, that's all.'

'Can't I come?'

'Not really, kiddo. Adult stuff.'

Adult stuff? What happened to him being a kid?

Like me.

Kwaku came out the gym door, his posh sports bag flung over his shoulder. Up close, he was even taller than I thought. Probably six foot. Taller than Dad – taller than Denny even.

Denny patted him on the back, put his hand on his shoulder. 'Just the man. Have you met my sister, Molly?'

Kwaku's teeth illuminated his face. 'Yeah. Got the bruise to prove it.' He rubbed his head, made a funny wincing face.

What a wimp.

I gave Denny the coldest stare I could find.

'Don't be shy, kiddo. Kwaku can give you the lowdown on the skills bouts, can't you, lad?'

Kwaku scratched the back of his head. 'Uh, yeah. I was just gonna get the bus, but we can chat on the way?'

I'd never seen anyone smile so much and it really annoyed me. I didn't want to be left with Happy Boy. I gave Denny my best puppy-dog eyes – the ones I reserve for mega situations. 'Denny, please . . . can I just come with you?'

'Sorry, kiddo. Tell Mum I'll be home in time for grub.' Then he turned to Kwaku, patted him on the back again. 'Be lucky, mate –' and with that he buggered off, leaving us there.

Kwaku started walking. 'You coming?'

I grunted. 'Fine.' I swung my tatty old Primark bag over my shoulder and followed him.

'You're well lucky having Denny as your brother. Everyone loves him,' said Kwaku.

'He's lucky too to have me as a sister.'

He nodded.
We walked a bit more
without chatting,
the sound of the traffic
humming all round us.
My head buzzed.
I wondered what to say.
My shoulders tensed,
so that they were almost
touching my ears.
I hated the awkwardness
of being with someone
I didn't know.
What do I say?
Ask him something, Molly.

Kwaku broke the silence before I had a chance. 'Must have been scary coming to the gym. I remember my first day – it was terrifying.'

We stopped at the pelican crossing. I pressed the button on the traffic light. Buses and cars whizzed by, the rumble of exhausts rattling the pavement under us. 'Nah, it was easy,' I said. 'I wasn't worried at all.'

'You must be pretty brave then.'

I willed the lights to go green, the traffic to stop. So we could keep moving, not be standing still. 'Denny says brave is doing something you're scared of. I wasn't scared.'

'Fair enough.' He smiled.

Finally, the *beep, beep, beep* of the traffic lights parted the cars, giving us permission to cross.

'You getting the bus?'

I nodded.

'What number?'

'86.' I hoped it wasn't the same one as him.

'Me too. We can get on together.'

DAMN!

I sat on the red shiny bus bench. Kwaku joined me. 'So how come you want to box?' he said.

'I dunno.' I'd never thought about why. I just knew it lived somewhere in the centre of me. Like, when Denny was teaching me boxing moves, or when I was watching him in the ring, all the noise went away. I wasn't just some girl off the estates any more. I was me. Molly Levine. It sometimes felt like boxing had crawled right up into my mind and lived there. But I wasn't going to tell Happy Boy that – I'd sound like a right blend.

'I just wanna be badass. And what's more badass than being able to punch proper hard?'

RUBBER MATCH

I rush through my front door. I need to let Kwaku know about our next lead.
 Seffi.
He might know what to do next.
I rush into my bedroom.
Stomp stomp stomp
  down the hallway.
'Where the hell have you been?'
Dad.
I close my eyes, wish him away. 'Just out on the estate.'
'Your mother's been worried sick.'
I look into the kitchen. Mum's sitting *exactly* where I left her that morning.
'She don't look that worried to me.'
'How could you?'
'How could I what, Dad?'
'Your poor mother – you know what she's going through. How could you make her worry like that?'

A flutter in my chest
building into an eruption.
What Mum's *going through? What about me? Anyway, what's made him the saviour all of a sudden? All he's ever done is mope around and sleep.*

I put a lid on it.

There's no point. Cos whatever he thinks, I don't want any more trouble.
'I was just seeing some mates. I'm sorry.'
'You're out having a laugh with mates, with all this going on?'

The lid blows off –
  I can't stop it.

'Stop having a go at me! It isn't easy on me either.'
Mum shuffles something in the kitchen.
Dad looks at me, like I'm something he's stepped in. 'I can't believe how

selfish you're being.' He turns back to the kitchen, shoulders slumped.

Anger . . . Boiling . . . Hot . . . Fury . . . Volcanic . . . Eruption . . .

. . . BLAST! –

'Well, I'm all you've got left. So get used to it, and actually, maybe Denny wouldn't be in trouble if you'd been less of a zombie. Maybe you should look at yourself for once, instead of blaming everyone else.' I turn round, my heart pounding out of my chest, and I leg it down the hallway, practically leap into my room. Close the door, hold my back against it, listen for his footsteps.

Ready to defend myself again.

Expecting him to follow, expecting him to come in and give me a piece of his mind.

But he doesn't,

and I feel proper guilty for what I said.

I chuck the books off my bed and pull the duvet up over me. It takes some of the chill of the day away.

There,

quiet.

Finally.

Duvets feel like safe spaces. Even in the summer, when it's blazing hot, I have a duvet. It's like a cuddle at the end of the day – and I defo need one of them, the way I'm feeling.

I plug my phone in and lean on my side so I can use it while it charges. I text Kwaku. I'm too stressed to call him and, anyway, if I did, he'd only ask me a million questions.

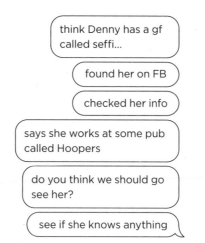

think Denny has a gf called seffi...

found her on FB

checked her info

says she works at some pub called Hoopers

do you think we should go see her?

see if she knows anything

One, two . . . ten seconds . . . my phone buzzes.

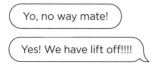

Yo, no way mate!

Yes! We have lift off!!!!

I shake my head. He's such a weirdo.

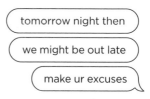

tomorrow night then

we might be out late

make ur excuses

I put my phone under my pillow, let thoughts of Denny, Seffi, that man beaten in the alley spin me in my bed.

I sleep.

THE COMEBACK

I sneak past Mum and Dad's room I don't want to wake Dad. I can't face running into him after last night.

Mum's in the kitchen.

'Can I stay out later tonight? Amana is having a girly night.' Amana's an old school friend I hardly speak to any more.

Mum nods, cracks a teeny smile. 'You make sure you have a good time. Here –' she goes in her purse, pushes a fiver across the table at me – 'get you an' Amana some chips or something. Chips is all right for a vegetarian, ain't it?'

I laugh, wonder what's brought on this sudden mood change. 'Of course it is, Mum. Chips is potato. Potato ain't meat, is it?'

She shrugs. 'S'pose not.'

She puts one arm round me, holds the other, with her fag, out away from me. She isn't wearing perfume. I'm not sure she's even been showering. But she still smells like Mum. I breathe in her scent.

'Just try and enjoy it, OK?' She pulls my hair from my face, tucks it behind my ears.

'I will. I gotta get to school now. You gonna be OK?'

'Never mind me. Have you had your breakfast?' She crosses her arms. She hasn't asked me about breakfast in yonks. She's nuts about eating breakfast, but I hate it. Usually, I put a few cornflakes and some milk in the bottom of a bowl and leave it in the sink, to trick her into thinking I've had it. But I've stopped bothering lately and she ain't noticed, up till now.

'Here –' she pushes another quid into my hand – 'grab yourself one of those French cwassun thing-a-ma-bobs.'

I take the money from her, feeling guilty cos I know she must be skint. 'You sure you don't need it?'

She scrunches her face like she's trying not to cry. 'Nah. Got one less to feed at the mo, ain't I? And, just like that, she's lost her spark again.

It's selfish, I know, but I've got bigger fish to fry – Seffi. 'I'm gonna be late, Mum. Better go.'

And I leave her there, just as she begins to cry.

FIGHTER OR SHRIMP?

After school I head straight to Duke's. Frank's been giving Kwaku gyp about not pushing himself hard enough (something I've heard said to me enough times, but mostly in maths) so I'm trying to lift his spirits.

Frank calls my name from his office. 'Hang on,' I shout, and turn back to Kwaku. 'Meet you in the changing room. Cheer up – we got a proper mission tonight.' I pat his arm.

Kwaku nods, not a smile in sight. It's so unlike him and it freaks me out.

I go over to Frank's office. 'What's up?' I say.

'Come in, Molly – sit down.'

The room stinks of coffee and fag ash. I sit on the crusty couch, opposite his desk. After the lecture that Kwaku's had from Frank, I think I'm going to be next. 'Have I done something wrong?'

'Nah, don't be silly. I just wanted you to know, I've been watching you. You've been working hard, and I reckon you could be ready to try for another bout.'

'What?'

'Another fight. I've got you on an undercard. I won't lie to you, you're probably gonna lose. It's not been long since your last bout. But it's about getting experience in the ring.'

My body feels like it's caving in and folding in half. 'I don't want to lose again. I ain't fighting until you know I'll win. It matters that I win.'

'Look, Molly . . .'

I feel the sparks inside me go off like crazy and from somewhere new. 'No,' I say, 'you look. I lost my first fight and I lost my brother. I'm not losing nothing else. I'll fight when I'm ready to win.'

Frank sits back really deep in his chair. 'Might be some time till that happens, Molly.'

'So what? I ain't in any rush. And what about Denny? I don't want him missing another one of my fights.'

Frank points to the gym outside. 'He could walk through that door any day. Do you want him walking back through it and seeing you as a fighter or a shrimp?'

The thought hurts my belly.

I feel a lump in my throat.

Even though I can't face
another loss.
He's right.
I have to fight.
For Denny.
For me.
To prove I'm a somebody.
But he's wrong too.
I *am* gonna win!

I nod. 'All right, I'll do it. But I want proper training, no half-arsed stuff.'
Frank winks. 'That's my girl.'

RUNNING

Running for the sake of it.
Again . . .
Bleurgh!
For football, yeah;
athletics, yeah.
But for fitness?

What a joke.

> 'Running keeps the heart ticking,
> gives you stamina,' said Denny.

Boring, boring, boring.
One hour, round the park
    every
      morning.

This wasn't boxing. This was prancing.
This was *booooooooooooring*!

> 'Let's stop,' I beg. 'This is hell.'

Denny flicks my ponytail.
    'You daft sod. Stop bloomin' moaning.'

I tutted.
    'If I wanted to be a flippin' runner,
    I'd've joined the Harriers.'
He droned on about stamina,
learning to breathe properly,
this and that,
    blah blah blah.

I stopped listening. I just wanted to be at Duke's,

fighting, boxing,
mowing people down.

He bent over, did his lace up.
'Last one to the school gate
is a blend!'
    He legged it—

Bleedin' moron,
didn't even wait.
    I ran after him,
feeling the energy run through me,
feeling the buzz of the blood
rushing round me
    even though running sucks.

HOOPERS

I've gone and borrowed one of Mum's dresses. It's black, skinny-fitting and low cut. I don't have boobs to fill it like Mum, so it just hangs off me like a bin bag. It's not the glamorous look I had in my head. I also took some stupid high heel shoes too that make me wobble like I'm a bloomin' baby taking my first steps.

Kwaku walks and I hobble across the road to Hoopers. He holds the door open for me. It's like he's my carer. I don't get why people wear dresses. I feel so bare, so exposed.

The music blasts.

It feels like everyone
is looking at us.
I stand out like a
sore thumb with
my flat chest and baggy dress.
I don't belong anywhere.

Trying to be laddish
in the gym – fail.

Trying to be womanly
in a bar – fail.

Trying to act swag
when I'm poor – fail.
I am a freak of nature.
Not this or that.
Not one nor the other. . .
Bleurgh.

'We should've got fake IDs.' I pull my dress down towards my knees, hating the feeling of my legs on show.

'*Shhh*, it'll be all right. Let's go sit down.'

We find a booth within eyeline of the bar, tucked away in the corner. I sit down. It's a relief to get off my wobbly feet. I look across, try to see if Seffi's there. But there's only one bloke, wiping down the bar.

'I can't see no woman. Maybe she ain't working tonight.'

'Be patient,' Kwaku replies. 'She might be having a break or starting later. I'll get some drinks.'

I grab his sleeve. 'You can't – they'll notice you.'

'They'll notice us more if we *don't* buy drinks.'

'What? Booze?' I say, worried he won't get served, even though he looks older than sixteen.

He gives me a funny look, like I'm an alien. 'I wish! But no way they're gonna serve me in here. It ain't Vic's Minimart. They'll ask me for ID.'

I let go of his sleeve. He goes to the bar, confident as you like, leaves me on my tod.

I feel so paranoid.
What if Dad's out drinking?
I shake my head.
No, this isn't his scene.
He goes to proper boozers,
not trendy bars
with boomy music
and cocktails.

And . . .

what if Mum
calls Amana's mum
and finds out
I'm not with her
and gets scared
I'm missing?

Guilt twists me in half.
I don't want to stress Mum.

'Here. Two Cokes. I got us ice and lemon too.' Kwaku puts the drinks down on the table. 'You all right? You look like you've seen a ghost.'

I sit up straight, pull my dress down over my knees, pretend to be fine. I want to look cool. Let things wash over me. Like Kwaku does. Mind you, if I was him, I wouldn't have this problem. I could go out and buy a brand-new dress that actually fits me, instead of scabbing one of Mum's.

So I say, 'Yeah, I'm cool, I'm good. Any sign of Seffi?'

'No, but it's still early.'

'You think no one's gonna notice us? Two kids pretending to be adults, sat here all night?' He really is the most naïve moron alive.

'Have some patience, will you? It's like when Muhammad Ali won Rumble in the Jungle. He waited and soaked up the punishment. He could've danced round and dodged, but he wanted Foreman to punch himself out. He only moved when he had to. He waited. And when Foreman was exhausted, Ali unleashed the bee sting. Bam!'

'Not everything's about Ali, you know?'

'Course it is. "Float like a butterfly, sting like a bee." Battles aren't just physical, they're mental too, innit?'

SLAM!

The table shudders.

A woman – black eyes, tattoos, piercings through her lips, nose and eyebrows – is looking down at us.

'Right, up and out, the pair of yous. What are you – like, ten years old?' She stares right at me. I freeze, have no idea what to say.

Seffi?

'No . . . uh . . . um . . . eighteen,' mumbles Kwaku.

'Between yous, maybe. Come on, let's be having you. You trying to lose Ross his licence, or get me sacked?'

It is Seffi.

There's no mistaking it.

She's the girl from the photo on Facebook.

She slaps both her hands down on the table again and I swear she growls. 'I ain't stupid, kid. We get plenty like you in here trying to get booze.' She picks up one of the Cokes and sniffs it.

I give her the puppy-dog eyes. 'It's not got nothing in it, honest.'

'Well, off with you both anyway.' She puts her hands on her hips, tuts. 'Don't make me get security.'

I doubt security would be scarier than her.

I get up, forgetting about the heels, and wobble, almost fall flat on my face. *It is her.*

I don't know what to do.

She wraps her arms across her chest, shifts her weight from one leg to the other. I can tell her left foot's weaker. If I wanted to, I could knock her over.

'Right.' She grabs us both by the arms, practically throws us towards the door.

I choke back the lump in my throat. I have to fight back, but with words instead of what I'm good at, my fists – 'Wait . . . wait! I'm Molly.'

'And I'm the Queen of Sheba. Now, out!'

She goes to grab me again, but this time I whack her hand out of the way. 'Denny's sister.'

Her lip quivers, and her body softens.

'I found you on Facebook. I need your help.'

Kwaku puts his hand on her arm, does one of his calm smiles. 'We really need your help. Please.'

Seffi bites her lip, sniffs back the tears and pats her hair into place. 'I've got a break at nine. Meet me in that all-night café, down by the station. Quarter past.' Her eyes go shifty. 'Just you twos – no one else. If I get even a sniff of the Ol' Bill, you're on your own.'

SEFFI'S SECRET

The café is a dive. On the table opposite us is some old drunk geezer, kipping against the wall. By the counter, a dodgy-looking bloke swearing at a fruit machine. It's cold and the lights are too bright.

'You sure we're safe in here?' I ask Kwaku.

'It'll be fine. He examines a sticky plastic menu.

'You gonna order anything?' asks a waitress out of the blue.

'Yeah, we're just waiting on our friend.' Kwaku tucks the menu back between the salt and pepper pots.

The waitress glares at him. Taps her pen on her notepad, one, two, three times. 'Well, this ain't no doss house. Ten mins. If you ain't ordered by then, you can sling your hook, the pair of you,' and she stomps off.

'Charming, ain't she?' I look at my phone. Nine twenty. 'She's late – she's probably changed her mind.'

'Nah, give her a chance.'

Just then, the door flings open. It's Seffi, sopping wet. She shakes her hair out like a dog, not giving two hoots that she's soaking the place. 'Jesus, this bleedin' weather! One minute hot, next minute cold. Now rain. Does me head in.'

She spots us. 'Go on then, shove over,' she says to Kwaku.

He gets up, all clumsy, knocks the chairs into each other.

Seffi sits down. Her cheap perfume's a nice change from the stink of grease. 'Oh, darlin'?' She waves at the waitress, who's now leaning against the counter, staring at her phone, but she looks up when Seffi calls, pulls out her pad and comes over. 'Your mate's real then.'

'I'm real, yeah. And what's got you? Face on you, tsk! Swear you was chewing a wasp.'

The waitress looks down her nose at Seffi, then glances over at a man behind the counter, who must be her boss, because she suddenly decides to give us her full attention and smiles.

Fake.

'What can I get you?'

Seffi pulls out a mirror, starts rubbing black mascara off her cheeks.

'Three Cokes please.'

The waitress scribbles it down, like it's something she could forget, then stomps off.

'Bundle of laughs, ain't she?' Seffi shakes her head.

'Haha, yeah.' Kwaku giggles, his eyes gooier than normal.

The waitress brings over three cans and three polystyrene cups. She slams Seffi's down hardest. Seffi smiles. 'Ta, darlin'.' The waitress glares at her, then marches off, her ponytail swinging behind her. One yank and I could have her on the floor, no problem.

Seffi clicks open her Coke and drinks it out of the can. 'Used to be much nicer in here, when Garbo ran it. I mean, yeah, it was only a front of house business –' she tapa her nose and winks, 'but at least it was proper.'

'Are you his girlfriend?' I ask.

She scrunches her face up. 'Yeah, I'm Denny's girl.'

'How come I ain't heard of you then?'

'It's complicated. All right?'

Kwaku jumps in. 'Do you know where Denny is?'

She rubs the corner of her eye, leans into her elbows. 'You didn't hear it from me, right?'

'Lips are sealed, innit, Molly?'

I smile through gritted teeth. 'Yup.'

'Cos if I find out yous said anything about me to anyone, even Denny, I'll bloody have you. Understand?' Her eyes are cold. Serious.

I nod. 'Yeah. We just want to find Denny. We don't want no trouble.'

'I don't know where he is, but I know he's safe.' She sits back again, like she's finished telling us the secret.

I lean forward, my heart in my belly. 'How do you know?'

'He told me. He's got people helping him. All I'm saying is, the answer is right under your noses.'

'What does that mean?' ask Kwaku.

'That's as much as I'm telling. I got to think of my protection too.'

I lean right into the table. 'Please, can't you tell us anything else? Cos you're not exactly being helpful.'

She smiles in that sad way that grown-ups do when they feel sorry for you. 'I've told you, he's safe, and I shouldn't have said even that.'

I lock her wrist in my hand, squeeze. 'Please . . . he's all I've got.'

She shrugs me off, holds my hand in hers. 'Kid, I want Denny back too. Believe me. But not as much as I want to keep my own safe, all right?' She pulls her soggy coat back on.

'But Denny *is* your own, ain't he? You said so yourself – you're Denny's girl.'

She yanks her phone out of her pocket, shoves it right in my face, so that my nose almost touches the screen. 'Not as much as he is.'

The drinks fridge hums, the coffee machine screeches. Coins clunk as the guy on the fruit machine wins the jackpot.

I let my eyes adjust. In front of me is a photo of Seffi cuddling a baby.

'Is he yours?' I ask, even though there's a different question playing through my mind.

'Every inch of him.'

MUHAMMAD ALI

A double decker pulled up. It was ours. I jumped up, got on first, found a seat upstairs and sat by the window. Kwaku shoved in next to me, his leg touching mine. Talk about awkward.

'I started boxing about a year ago,' he said, tucking his Oyster card into his back pocket.

I rubbed steam off the window with my sleeve, peered out into the dark wintery night. The street was chock-a-block full of buggies, street sellers, people walking God knows where. This is London.

Never a minute of silence or stillness; nothing ever stopping.

Just how I like it.

'Duke's is the second gym I've been to. We moved here in the summer, just before I started Year Eleven, then I met Frank, which was pretty epic.'

'Is he a good coach?' My curiosity got the better of me.

'Yeah, man's a legend.' He checked his phone. It was the latest iPhone. Must have cost a packet. He huffed, put it back in his pocket. 'Want to know why I started boxing?'

'Do I have a choice?'

'Cos I want to be as epic as Muhammed Ali, obviously!'

'Fat chance of that! He was a legend – you're just some kid from the East End.'

'Hey, man's got to dream and, anyway, I love it. I feel like I might be good at it. Never really bothered with footy, like most lads did. But boxing – yeah, it's my little space in the world.'

I sat up straighter, wrinkled my nose at him. 'What kind of a boy don't like football?'

'Me!' He slapped his hand against his chest, like he was the proudest person in the whole world.

What a melt.

I looked out through the window again. We were caught in heavy traffic, little red and amber lights creeping up the road as far as my eyes could see.

The bus sped up a bit, then stopped again. Kwaku pressed the bell, stood up. 'This is my stop. See you at Duke's.' He got up, swung himself round the rail and disappeared down the stairs and into the street.

As the bus pulled off, I looked down, watching to see what way he went.

It looked like he was going towards the new flats at Flock Heart Rise.

Tut. Those were the flats that were built over the old estates. Hundreds of people, families going back generations, real cockneys, chucked out of their homes, split up and forced to be hidden away in places like Essex. Dad said it was called 'gentrification' – in other words, skimming off the scum. There'd be no cockneys left soon, Dad said.

We're a dying breed.

EXCUSES

I got to the gym first thing,
cos I had to get some
      energy out.

Every last bit of my
      stupid
body burns.

My knees ache,
and my shoulders are
agony.

Even the palms of my hands
are sore with sweat.

      'Focus, Molly. Look.
      Hands up. Like this. Here.'

Frank shoves my left hand,
over my cheek.
    'Come on, *focus.*'

    FOCUS
       is
    impossible.

    Focus

       Focus

      Focus
Anyway, what does it matter?
I suck. BIG TIME.

The crease in my arm aches.
I try to shake the pain away.

It's too much.
Nobody can work this hard.
I'm not a blinkin'
     machine.
I'm *never* gonna win
this stupid fight.

It's pointless.

     'Come on, get those fists up.'
         Hands up
         Hands w~o~b~b~ly
         Hands
              flop.

     'Chest stiff and knees loose.
     How many times have I gotta tell you?'

I shift my hips, feel like a prize idiot, take a gander round the gym. Everyone's busy doing their own thing. Tiff and Chas are sparring in the ring; Duffy's skipping. The only eyes on me are those of the boxers in the posters on the walls.

The words *under your noses*
     buzzes round and round my head like a bad itch.
What the hell is it supposed to mean?
I take a long breath.
Try again.

My legs wobble, too weak to hold the stance. I whack at a tear in the punchbag, hoping it will rip in half and I'll be sent home. But, instead, pain rattles through me.

'I can't do it. I'm bleedin' useless. I hurt, I'm thirsty and my face is itching.'

Frank steadies the punchbag. 'So what if you hurt? Grab hold of that pain and thrash it out of you. Pain ain't real, it's a state of mind.' He clicks his fingers at me. 'Again.'

He is a monster.

I get back in my stance, rub the sweat off my head with my forearm. Left foot pointing forward, right foot steady, knees loose.

Fix my eyes on the punchbag.

> *Come on, come on,*
> > *let it out.*

I want so much for the boxing to take away the noise inside me.

Why won't Seffi tell me more? And that baby . . . if she was his girlfriend, is that baby his?

I want the boxing to help me escape, like Kwaku said it does for him.

I shake my head, as if to shake Denny away, and try again, crunch my fists into the tatty old punchbag.

CRUNCH *denny* Crunch *denny* crunch
Denny crunch *DENNY Denny, Denny, Denny, Denny Slap.*

Gah!

I kick the punchbag – *thud*. It swings back at me. Frank catches it, before it topples me over.

> I pound my head
> against the bag.
> My chest heaves,
> each breath forces
> the stench of sweat
> into my mouth.
> It tastes rank.

> 'I can't do it. My body's falling apart.'

Need water.
I wriggle off my glove.
It squeaks with sweat.

'There's no such thing as "can't".
When life hits you, you hit back harder.'

He sounds like he's straight out
of a boxing movie.

It's embarrassing.

I grab my drink bottle, glug,

        glug,

          glug.

Scratch my face like crazy.

'Denny wouldn't have wanted you faffing like this. He'd have wanted you getting on with it.'

Wouldn't have?

Like Denny's in the past?

I pull my head back, squirt more water in my gob. The brightness of the neon lights pierces my eyes. I ram the lid back on the bottle. Square up to Frank. 'Denny – is – not – dead.'

'I didn't mean it like that.' The wrinkles in his face turn upside down.

I chuck my bottle on the floor, flex my hand and drag the glove back over my clammy skin. 'Anyway, Denny would be gutted if I forgot about him. Everyone keeps saying Denny wants me to be happy, but if I went missing and everyone was having a laugh – not sad or missing me – I'd be well gutted.' I know it sounds harsh, but I don't care – it's true. Adults spend so much time pretending. Never saying the proper truth. I'll never be like that.

Frank shrugs, huffs. 'I dunno, Molly, maybe you're right.' He looks at his watch. 'Let's wrap it up for today, eh?'

I whack the punchbag proper hard. 'You giving up on me?'

'Don't be so soft. You deserve a break. Here –' he pulls his wallet out and shoves me a fiver. It brushes off my glove and lands on the concrete floor.

'I don't want bribing. I want to fight. I want to win. Win for Denny.'

Frank pushes the punchbag. The chain attaching it to the ceiling clanks. It echoes round the room.

The whack, whack, whack on the bags.

Swoosh.

The urgh, urgh, urgh.

Grunts.

No wonder I can't focus.

'Do you really want to box?' Frank asks. 'Cos it feels like I'm wasting my time.'

'Yes. I do.'

'Molly, look . . . boxing ain't just about turning up physically. You've got to turn up in your head too. It's for those who want to win. It's for those who see bad things in the world and want to destroy them.' Frank is giving up on me.

'I do want to win,' I insist. 'It's just hard . . . you even said it yourself – I'm never gonna win this fight.'

'Life's hard, Molly. It'll boot you down, crush you and rip you to pieces. But there's two types of people. The ones who let life break them by moaning and being bitter, and the ones who stare life in its ugly mug and tear it in half. You've got to be the one who stands up after the knock-down and gets up fighting harder. Only you can do that. But you've gotta do it for yourself. Ain't no other person gonna get you your dreams. That's down to you and only you.'

I nod. 'I do, I do want to win, for me. I'm a fighter and I'm ready.' A lump creeps up into my throat. I bit my lip to stop it shaking. I'm not ready at all. I don't believe in the dream, just like Dad doesn't. Maybe I should just give up.

Frank shakes his head. 'Nah, Molly, you're here cos you enjoy being angry. Angry about your lot in life, then about Denny. What's your next reason gonna be? As far as I can see, you're comfortable with excuses, cos it means you don't have to try. And if you don't try, you can't fail, and that's the heart of it. That's what you're scared of.'

'It's just been so hard . . .'

He shakes his head again. 'Denny never gave up and he was happy as Larry, even though he was going through hell trying to look after you and that mum of yours. Never saw that boy with a sour look on his face, not once.'

My chest explodes. 'If he's so good at looking after us, where is he?' I'm shouting, saying things out loud I've not even said to myself.

Frank just shakes his head again.

'Frank, please.'

'Sorry, kid. You're on your own. I've got enough on my plate.' He marches off to his office and slams the door with a bang.

It isn't a test. He actually flippin' means it.

Tiff and Chas are looking at me. 'What you bogging at?' I cry.

Chas makes a funny face, then goes back to punching Tiff's mitts.

Frank's words bang inside my head, like a fist to the skull.

You're on your own.

T-REX

Kwaku is sitting on the locker room bench lacing up his boots.

I chuck my gloves in my locker and pull on my hoodie. It's filthy with stains and has a hole in the front.

'What's up?' Kwaku comes over and rests a hand on my shoulder.

I drag my hood up to hide my face, lean my head against the grey metal locker. It's cold against my hot skin. I can't face him right now. I close my eyes, hope he'll go away.

'Oi, Molly.' He clicks his fingers at me, trying to bring me back to earth.

He ain't going to give up. I bite my lip hard, hoping the pain will stop me crying. 'Him in there –' I nod towards Frank's office – 'he just lost it with me.'

'Oooh, what did you do?'

'Why assume it's my fault? He's a bloomin' moron. Reckon he's got proper anger issues.'

Kwaku huffs, slumps back against the locker. 'I heard on the grapevine that guy – Harry Wilson – might not recover from his coma. Frank's stressed that it's bad news for Duke's. Publicity or something. Suppose he won't be up for my training session then.'

What does this mean for Denny? Will Ol' Bill think he's a murderer now?

'We need to go visit Harry, see if we can find out anything from his family or something.'

'Are you sure that's a good idea?'

'It's not like we have any other leads, and this could get even more serious for Denny if we don't do something about it.'

'True.'

The room feels smaller, the music louder. I want out of here. I shove myself off the locker and pull at Kwaku's sleeve. 'You want to go to the chicken shop? Frank just chucked me a fiver.'

'Sorry, I've gotta train, Frank or no Frank. Need to keep up my stamina.'

I want out of Duke's, but I don't fancy going home either. I pull him again. 'Come on, just this once. Imagine them tasty chicken wings dripping with peri-peri sauce.'

He drags his teeth along his bottom lip. 'Mate, even if I had time, I've gotta watch my diet. But, hey, why don't you stay? You've your own fight in a few weeks, you can't afford to slack neither.'

'I'm gonna lose anyway. Frank's given up on me.'

'Nah, he's just stressed.'

'He reckons I'm a loser.' I pick at the paint on the locker door. Like everything else in Duke's – in my life – it's a crusty, worn-out mess.

'You want to prove him wrong?'

I do. More than anything, but what's the use? 'I'm done in, mate. My arms kill and, every time I throw a punch, my knees go hard – I keep forgetting to keep them loose. Then there's these stupid itches on my face that I can't get at, cos scratching with gloves on is proper hard, and I want to let my anger out, but there's so much I'm mad about I dunno where to start. Frank says my rhythm's useless. But I feel like a melt bouncing round, hitting stuff that ain't there. I don't lose on purpose. Losing just happens to me.' I pull my hood off my head. 'People like me . . . ? You wouldn't understand. I was born to lose.'

Tiff comes in, a towel slung over her toned shoulders. 'Don't be daft, you silly mare. Nobody's born to lose. I'm straight off the estates and I've got where I am through pure hard work and determination. You just gotta want it, love.' She disappears into the showers.

Tiff's off the estates.

I had no idea.

Kwaku turns to face me. 'Tiff's right – you're not a loser. A pain in the butt – yeah, maybe, but not a loser. You just need to find your thing. Like, for me, rap helps with rhythm. Since I started using it, my footwork is way better.'

'What? Rap music?'

'Yeah, like, you know, JME or the master, Skepta.'

'What the bleedin' heck has that got to do with fighting?'

'You know . . . it's got a beat – like boxing does, innit?'

'How?'

'It kind of sings. You know . . . you can move to it, and if you can move to it, you can box to it, cos boxing's like dancing. Why'd you think they play it in the gym? It psychs the blokes up.' He clears his throat. 'Ladies too.' He nudges his shoulder into mine.

'Well, it don't do nothing for me and I ain't no lady.'

'That's cos you aren't listening. Not your strongest point, is it? I'll show you if you want.'

'What?'

'How to dance.'

'Dance? Nah, you're not my type. I don't fancy geeks.'

'Very funny. Come on, you'd be doing me a favour. It'll help me revise my technique.'

I know it'll be pointless, but I really don't want to go home, and Kwaku ain't going to stop nagging, so I shrug. 'Fine, whatever, but I'm telling you, it's pointless.'

'Epic! Let's go in the sparring room. It's empty and there's a mirror for shadow boxing.'

I grab my gloves back out of my locker. 'But there ain't no speakers for music in there.'

He laughs. 'Who needs speakers? Man spits his own bars, innit?'

'You?'

He nods, smiling his stupid beaming smile at me.

This I have to hear.

'Close your eyes. I want you to focus on my voice. No talking. Actually listen. I need you to find that drive in you to box. Frank calls it the fire in your belly. Think of the angriest thing you can think of. Who do you want to rip apart . . . swear at . . . ? What's hurt you most?'

Being born broke.

'Got something in your head? Good. Now use that person to push through the pain. When you feel it, think how you're gonna beat it and, with every punch, you're gonna take away one of those things.'

Dad. Get a job,
Going to food banks,
Having to steal Mr Weaver's WiFi,
Being brassic . . .
Denny, why did you leave me?—
What? No.
Not Denny.
It's being on the breadline
I'm angry at.
Stupid, stupid poverty.
Having to wear this
non-brand gear,
whilst everyone else at Duke's
is proper kitted out.

'This thing's hurt you. So, you gotta hurt it. Get revenge.'

Revenge,
Show them what I'm made of.
Sod
being poor,
being hungry,
being cold,
being a nobody.
Not Denny.

'Set yourself up in your stance, get comfy, pull your left hand back over your face, protect yourself, loosen your knees. Yeah, yeah – good.'

Not Denny.
Not Denny.
Not Denny.
It's the unfairness of the world.

'Now come forward, like nobody gonna see you coming, one step at a time, like you're stalking your prey . . . Good! Now two back . . . Yeah, yeah.'

Denny –
why did you tell Seffi and not me?

Two right.
Two left.

Denny –
is she more important than me?

'Awesome! Now turn yourself on your back foot, like, spin, yeah – good good! Footwork's not half bad – just got to connect it with your upper body.'

Denny –
I thought I was your number one.

'Time to rip them apart. Show me what you've got. Throw some punches.'

Denny—
> *Denny.*
> *Denny.*
> *It's bleedin' Denny*
> *I'm angry at.*
Not being poor.
Not being a nobody.

> *I'm not a nobody at Duke's.*
> *Tiff's right. We all bleed*
> *red, no matter where*
> *we're from.*

'Woah! Not that fast – it isn't a race! Throw one punch and rest. Sit yourself into your stance . . . that's it, now throw another . . . right, now try a few in a row. Rest between shots, make sure your elbows aren't too wide. Pull them in . . . that's it.'

> *Denny did a runner.*
> *Denny left me.*
> *Denny, are you*
> *dead or alive?*

> *Did you hurt that Harry?—*
> *No, throw that out your*
> *head – now!*

'God, girl! You're holding your breath so bad you're gonna suffocate. Breathe!'

> *I breathe.*
> *It clicks.*
> *Tumbles out of me.*
> *I'm a machine.*

'One, two . . . One, two, one . . . One, two . . . OK. . . . Defence now – bob and weave, bob and weave, then back in the punching position. Here's the rhythm. You've got to imagine yourself loose. Feel the beat go through you. Like music—

Remember your knees.
Duck, right, jab left.
Duck left, jab right.
Amazing! You're ready.

Keep your eyes closed and listen. Feel what I say, feel my beats. Breathe it in. Like a heartbeat – *bom boom, bom boom*. Feel the power in your back foot with each jab. Dance, yeah? Here goes—'

She's from East London,	*duck left*
man calls her carnivore . . .	*jab left—*

Oi, it's not funny. *Focus*. Back in the stance. *Again!*

She's from East London,	*duck left*
man calls her carnivore,	*jab left*
watch out, cos she's	*duck right*
gonna smash in your front door!	*jab right . . .*

Good, good – now do it with confidence. Again! This time with hooks . . .

Stronger with her left fist,	*duck left*
call her South Paw,	*Hook left*
no problem	*duck right*
knocking bruv on the ring floor!	*hook right . . .*

You got it – don't stop. Feel the beat. Pull that hook round. Imagine punching them in the ear – the ear is one of the most painful places you can get punched. Right, go . . .'

'One, two –
her uppercut will make your jaw sore.
Three, four –
got more records than Spotify.
Better be sure,
Molls sees so much red –
last night she scared a matador!'

'Check you the hell out! Girl's on fire! Wait for it, ahem . . . Ladies and gentlemen! In the blue corner, I give you Molly "T–Rex" Levine!'

'Girl's a tyrannosaur,
you better watch her roar – *raaah*!'
And yeah, I actually
start to feel good.
Guard up, elbows in,
knees loose.
I'm not a loser.
Jab, jab –
    focus.

I empty.

Uppercut –
jab, jab –
    focus.
No pain.
No pain.
No pain.
FOCUS.
    I *will* win.

                CRUNCH

            Crunch

        Crunch

crunch

     ROAR   ROAR   ROAR

Tyrannosaur
       Tyrannosaur
             Tyrannosaur
                 Tyrannosaur

I SEE YOU

Harry Wilson is
in a side room.
Daffodil ward,
third floor.

We peer through
the window.
He's wired up,
tubes in his
mouth.

Battered.

A man comes to
the door, opens it.

'Can I help you?'
We stare blankly.

Both of us shocked
at the state of Harry.

He looks at me
real carefully.

'You're that Levine's
sister, ain't you?'

'I just wanted to ask—'
He slams the door,
right in our faces.
What a waste of
        time.

LIONESS

My gaff is freezing. We must have run out of leccy on the electricity key and Mum hasn't got enough cash to top it up. Looks like we're in for another night of double duvets and jumpers. I chuck my bag under my bed, hear voices from down the hall, go to investigate. The Old Bill are questioning my folks in the kitchen, again.

I rush in, thinking they've found him. 'Is everything all right? Have you found Denny?' I ask the police lady, who looks too old to do a job where running might be involved.

Mum flicks her hand at me. 'Molly, go to your room. I'll come see you in a minute.'

'But . . .'

Dad pipes up. 'Go on, Molly. It's nothing to worry about, baby.'

Why's he being so nice suddenly?

The woman police officer looks at her male colleague, gives me a pitying look, like I'm some poor fragile thing that needs protecting.

I huff. 'Fine.' If I make a scene, throw my weight round, I'll show them how angry I am. I leave them to it, but I keep the kitchen door ajar so I'll be able to sneak a listen from the other side. I stomp heavily to my room, make sure my bedroom door slams hard, then tiptoe back up the hallway towards the kitchen.

I peer through the narrow gap, squinting my eyes tight so I can see better and focus harder on what they're saying. Mum's sitting at the dinner table. The police officers are opposite her. I can't see Dad through the tiny gap – he must be over by the sink.

'You know, if we find out you're hiding him,' the woman is saying, 'you could both get into a lot of trouble. This could quickly go from GBH to a murder charge.' I squint my eyes a bit more. 'And the types your Denny hangs round with – it's likely he's been in danger. You wouldn't want that on your conscience now, would you?'

What does she mean? Who has Denny been hanging around with? Maybe that's how he got the gloves. *Is he involved with the wrong people?* I think back to that first day I got the bus with Kwaku and he said he had to run some 'errands'. He seriously didn't want me coming with him. Was he off with some dodgy people then?

'Way I see it, truth always comes out in the end, Mrs Levine,' the man says. 'And you've got to think of your girl in there. Wouldn't want social services getting involved and whatnot.'

They weren't even bothering to talk to Dad. Just laying it on thick with Mum. As if they think she's weaker cos she's a woman. But I know deep down he's the weak one.

'We dunno nothing,' says Mum, her voice growing angry. 'I dunno how many times we've got to tell you – if we knew where he was, we'd be with him.' She's so fierce I almost feel sorry for the coppers. 'My Denny ain't no murderer. You should be trying to find him to make sure he's all right, not coming here accusing him!' Dad's hand appears on Mum's back. She looks over at the door – I duck back. There's more talking, but I daren't get too near the gap. I can tell it's the woman talking. I shuffle my ear closer, keeping myself out of sight.

My heart pounds.

'Well, we've done all we can. Way I see it is this – when we find your boy, he's going down for a very long time. It don't look good, Mrs Levine, and if his victim don't wake up, well, things could get even more serious. Perhaps you might like to think about that.'

Mum stands up, slams her hands on the table, leans into the copper's face. 'You think I ain't thought about it? You think just cos we live in this place, cos we ain't got no money, cos we don't have clever jobs, come from fancy places, that we ain't good parents? I raised that boy well. He's got a heart of gold. Raised my girl well too. They got manners and they know right from wrong – all any mother could ask for. You – you've got the nerve to say you've done all you can? You're just trying to save face and boost your blinkin' numbers. *He's* not bad. *You* are. He could be lying in a ditch for all you know. Get out there and do your bleedin' job! Find my boy and stop harassing me. Or else I'll phone the papers and tell them about how the police like bullying those what's less fortunate.'

The coppers don't stand a chance with Mum now.

'We'll be seeing you, Mrs Levine,' says the policeman and they start to turn towards the door.

I rush back to my room, jump on my bed, ruffle the blanket round me to make it look like I've been there the whole time.

Footsteps fill the hall. The front door clicks. But nobody comes to check on me.

Lying in bed, I think about Mum shouting, standing up for us, not taking any rubbish. Mum's a lioness who's not going to let anyone hurt her cubs.

I get up, go to the kitchen, force a fake smile, sure they'd seen me and know I'd been listening.

'All right, love?' Mum starts pulling out pans from the cupboard like nothing's happened. She's got on a huge jumper (Mum suffers the most with the cold when we can't afford heating). 'Fancy egg and chips? Dad brought home some ham an' all. Let's treat ourselves, eh?' A cold puff of air escapes her mouth, she rubs her hands together, a shiver wobbles over her shoulders.

I look at Dad. His face cupped in his hands.

'Yeah, that'd be nice, Mum,' I say.

She comes over, kisses me on the head and, with the faintest of twinkles in her eyes, says, 'It's gonna be all right, baby. Just you see.'

I Facebook message Seffi.

Is Denny mixed up with any wronguns?

Wait, wait, wait . . .
Ping.

Don't be daft. He's salt of the earth that boy.

And she's right. He is. Denny is proper. He doesn't suffer bad guys gladly. Salt of the bleedin' earth.

Back to square one.

GLASS JAW

I'm meant to be meeting Kwaku to plan our next move in the search for who Denny is mixed up with. But the melt ain't turned up.

I wander towards his gaff, hope to bump into him halfway.

Nope.

Before I know it I'm on his estate.

Flock Heart Rise is proper posh. All glass buildings and shiny new stuff. There's a car park that goes under the building, and all the balconies have flowers and chairs, and some have even got barbecues. The gate at the front is taller than me. I stroll up to it and it opens on its own. Like, literally, I don't have to press a button or anything. It's mental, as if rich people shouldn't have to make an effort opening gates cos they've got better things to do with their time.

Talk about another bloomin' world!

I walk into the porch. It's clean and sparkly, no stench of pee or rubbish chutes. No abandoned settees or old mattresses. It smells like plastic and flowers and the lights are bright. It feels like I've walked onto a spaceship or into a testing lab. It isn't homely in the slightest, and everything looks the same. I see why Kwaku likes my estate. There's nothing here for your eyes to get interested in.

I press down on the intercom. It's digital, with blue electric numbers and a greeting that says WELCOME. Bleedin' heck, even the machines are polite. A man in a suit, holding a coffee in his hand, rushes past. Head down, he doesn't even look at me. I wonder if I should turn round. I don't belong in a place like this. Just being here makes me feel dirty, even though I had a shower this morning. But I have to see Kwaku. We need to investigate some more. I take a deep breath and press his number into the intercom.

'Hello?' a woman answers.

'Uh, yeah, is Kwaku there?'

'Just a minute.'

I stare at the blue letters on the screen, wait for his voice to come out of the speaker. The door to the main building clicks and Kwaku appears on the stairs in front of me. There's sadness painted thick on his face. He looks like he's been twelve rounds with an opponent five times his weight.

'Cor blimey, you look a sorry state,' I say.

'What do you want, Molly?' Not a smile in sight.

'We was meant to meet an hour ago, dummy? I got a lead, remember?'

'Right.' He rolls his eyes. He obviously doesn't want me here. 'Molly, I've got a lot going on.'

I can't believe it!

Too busy.

'But, we're partners, ain't we? In it together. I can't do it without you.'

He won't even look me.

'Are you all right? You don't look too sharp.'

'I've gotta go.' He climbs back up the stairs. No explanation.

Why is he being like this? What've I done wrong?

I look round at the fresh shininess of the place and I now I get it. He's ashamed of me coming to his gaff. He's fine being mates with a skank like me, as long as nobody from his shiny world sees me. Before I can stop myself, fury unloads itself out through my mouth.

'I knew you was like the rest of them – sitting up here in your flippin' castle, drinking your hazelnut coffees, with your shiny white Nike trainers and your brand-new iPhone. Too good for me, are you? Fine! Be like that. I don't need you anyway. I don't need no one. I'll stick to my own from now on.' I stick my middle finger up at him and stomp off, my heart almost ripping in two. My chest hurts. I want to run after him, tell him I'm sorry, tell him I don't mean any of it. But I keep walking. Like. A. Stubborn. Bleedin'. Idiot.

I need the gym.
I need focus.
Strength.
I need to get
Kwaku's sad eyes
out of my head.
I need to keep
my mind fresh.
I can't afford
to be a mess.
I've got a lead
to follow.

I don't need Kwaku anyway.

I put on my training gloves, start pounding the bag.

'Oh, that right hook's looking better than ever.'

It's Frank. 'Thought you'd had enough of me,' I say grumpily.

'Listen, Molly. I was too hard on you the other day. Can you forgive me?'

I'm not in the mood for him.

'I ain't promising you're gonna win this next fight.'

I want to tell him to naff off. 'I ain't fighting till Denny's back.'

Frank takes off his hat, presses it to his chest. 'Molly, have you thought maybe Denny ain't coming back?'

I catch the punchbag in my arms, stop it swinging and give him proper evils.

'You're wrong.'

Whack.

'This could go on eating you up for years. This thing with the bloke in the coma – I dunno, maybe Denny—'

'Don't even say it!'

Whack, whack.

'OK. Just think about it though. Denny would've loved you to keep boxing. You carry him wherever you go.'

What cheesy rubbish. I pound the bag again. It sounds like he's saying Denny is in heaven. I ain't into all that crap. I don't believe in God. Who would? If God is real, no way would he have done this.

Whack, whack, whack.

Frank puts his hat back on and slinks back to his office. He's wrong. Denny isn't gone and he is innocent. He's just too much of a wuss to face the music and tell the Old Bill he's innocent.

How dare Frank! *I'm gonna give him a proper piece of my mind!*

I storm towards his office, rage racing round my brain. But I can hear him raging at someone. Feeling nosy, I peer through the glass. He's on the phone, his face sort of panicky. I put my ear to his door, which is open a crack.

'I got coppers breathing down my neck. I'll see you tonight. Keep your head down.'

It sounds pretty suss.

There's a stirring in my belly.

A hunch.

Gut feeling.

I have to follow him.

SHADOWS

I sit at the bus stop outside Vic's shop across the road from Duke's and wait for Frank to appear. It's getting on, but still busy. The rush of traffic never stops round here. Just keeps humming and spitting and rumbling, all through the day and night. When I get home, Mum will go spare with me for being out so late. But I can't let that worry me. I might have an opportunity here to find out who did Harry Wilson over in the alley and I ain't gonna let that pass me by. I need to know what Frank is hiding and I need to know *now*.

A blue car's parked on the corner. A woman looks out, smiles at me, then looks away. I check my phone – 20:33. I've been waiting two hours already.

By nine thirty, I'm starting to give up.

Ten, Frank comes out.

Finally.

He keeps his face hidden inside a hoodie. Weird. I've never seen him in one before. He defo has something to hide.

I pull my scarf over my face, terrified he'll notice me, then carefully get up and pace after him. This is a covert operation, like real detectives do.

The woman in the blue car looks at me again.

I give her a stinking look. Nosy cow.

For an old man, Frank is fast and it's hard work keeping up with him. Kwaku would love this. I think about giving him a bell, to tell him the chase is on, but I ain't got time for that.

I need to keep my nerve.

Frank stops, swings a left onto Daster Road. I feel myself slowing down.

Daster Road is where the proper dodgy people live. Mum always tells me never to go down here, cos it's too dangerous. 'You'll end up coming home in an ambulance or – worse – a bleedin' coffin,' she says.

My belly fizzes. Now I really wish I had Kwaku with me. *Maybe I should give up. Go home. Stay safe. Listen to Mum.* But then again this could be my only chance. It's now or never. I rehearse some moves in my head.

One – jab, two – jab.

One – swing, two – jab jab.

One – upper cut, two – swing swing . . .

I'll be fine. The hospital and coffin scenario might be true for some people, but I'm a boxer.

I'm Tyrannosaur.

I'm Molly Levine and I'm gonna solve the case.

I'm gonna save my brother.

I zip up my hoodie, pull it up over my head, and turn into Daster Road. There's something about the place. A bad feeling hanging all over it. The air feels heavier, making the hairs on my neck stand up. People stand around on corners, sit on the pavements, and every single one of them stares at me as I pass, like they know I don't belong down here, like I'm intruding on their space. Like they want to proper hurt me. The smell of weed radiates from every corner. Such a nasty place. I keep my head down, one eye on Frank ahead, one hand on my phone, just in case I need to call the Old Bill.

We walk past a manky old park. A bunch of teenagers are shouting at each other and throwing each other about. Probably just play fighting, but it looks proper rough.

I feel like I need to get out of here, before I get hurt. But I might not get a chance like this again . . .

I shake my head.
Stand tall.
Rehearse my moves
in my head again.

Jab
swing
duck
dive
whack –
guy's a goner!

Frank turns into a front garden. Takes his keys out and goes into a big old Victorian house.

I stop. Pretend to look at my phone again, being careful nobody mugs it off me. I think about my next move. Is Denny in there? Should I knock on the door? Break in? A car pulls up a few metres away. I turn away, not wanting to bring attention to myself.

I'll text Kwaku. I flick his name up, but a stubborn voice deep inside of me says,

No,

you don't need him.
You can do this
> on your own.

My phone pings.
It's Mum.

> Where ru? It's gone 10 o'clock! Get home now!

I go to text her back, but just then my phone starts ringing. It's her. The ringtone belts out, sounding what feels like five thousand times louder than usual. The curtain in the house twitches. I duck down behind the front wall.

Press reject on my phone.

It rings again.

Whatever Frank is up to,

it's gonna have to wait.

SNUFFED

I dream of
Daster estate,
dream I'm in a fight
with one of the teenagers
in the park there.

Dream of a knockout
but I am the one
being knocked down.

My cheeks are crushed
into the gravel,
blood painting the cracks.
I look up.
There's the shadow of Denny,
watching
but not helping.

I cry out
but he just
takes a puff of his fag,
throws it down,
stamps it out,
walks away.

Then Seffi's standing over me.
She blows dust in my face,
whispers

Right under
your nose.

WINDOWS

The winter light is fast fading to dark. I've come to Daster estate straight from school. It's still early, so there's less chance of Mum being worried this time.

There's light peeping out from the front window, but the curtains are closed, so I can't see inside.

An alley runs alongside the left of the house.

I take a gander down there, but it's too dark to see where it goes – maybe it's a way to the back of the house? I look up and down the street, make sure no one's watching. It's empty. The coast is clear. Not wanting to risk the gate squeaking, I swing my leg up over the front wall, scramble over, and duck down, making myself small. Then I jig myself across the space of the front garden, the crunch of my trainers on the gravel sounding louder than a fog horn, but I get to the back fence and crouch against it. My heart thumps, cold fills my chest. I look back to the street to see if anyone's there.

Nothing.
Deep breaths,
puff, puff, puff.
Thank God!

I shuffle myself up and, keeping my back against the wall, edge my way along. Something scuffles ahead of me. Something big. I hold my breath. I've been caught!

I stand still as a statue.

A figure pounces out from under the fence—

Meow!
A blimmin' cat!
I almost laugh.
Pull yourself together, for God's sake.
Come on, Molly,
you can do this.

I rehearse my boxing moves again

Jab
duck
whack

and continue edging along. I don't dare move my head away from the wall or make a sound.

The wall changes from brick to . . . what is it? Wood? A handle. I turn round quick. Take a gander. It ain't padlocked or anything. It can't be this easy, surely? I put my hand on it and just hold it there, scared to turn it, scared it won't open, but scared it will too.

I close my eyes . . .

Clunk.

It clicks open right away. I slide into the back garden, my moves slick, like a puma, and shut the gate – real slow and gentle – behind me. I lean against the other side of the gate and close my eyes. Relieved I've made it into the garden. Not having the foggiest what my next move is going to be.

The
boom,
boom,
boom,
of my heart bounces in my head.

I open my eyes.
Blink a little to
adjust to the light.

Through the blinks
a figure appears
in the window.

The weight of everything
falls from me, my legs
turn to jelly.
I collapse.
It's Denny.

SAY SOMETHING

'Denny!' I shout, not caring how much noise I make. '*Denny!*' I run to the back door. Tears sting my eyes, my throat, my chest. The whole world's suffocating me. 'Denny, it's me!' I pound the door –

BANG BANG BANG!

'I've found you! Denny, Denny – Den! Open up – it's me! It's Molly.'

BANG BANG BANG!

'Answer the door, Den.' I kick the door.

BOOM BOOM BOOM!

The kitchen light goes off.
I hear the front door slam.
'Denny!'
He wouldn't have gone . . . would he?
No.

Any minute now,
he's gonna answer the door
and give me a massive cuddle.

Any minute now.

I wait.
Wait.
Wait.
Why isn't he coming? What's he playing at?
'Denny, I know you're in there. Please.'
              BANG
         BANG BANG
    BANG BANG BANG.

'DENNNNNNNNY!!!'

Nothing.

     Nothing at all.

I don't know what to do. I know he's in there. I'd seen him clear as day. Through that kitchen door, he'll have heard me. Why's he ignoring me? I don't get it. I've found him and I still can't get to him. Only a door separates us. I just want to get in there. Get to him – hold him, see that he's real, see his stupid dimple smile, call him a weirdo, let him ruffle my hair . . . tell me it's gonna be OK.

He has to come out.
He has to.

     I knock again –

          tap tap –

               quietly this time.

'Denny, please. Whatever's going on, we'll fix it. I'm sorry. Please, Denny . . . please . . .' My voice cracks and my body caves in with the pain of it all. It's all too much. I slump to the ground, sit my back up against the door, bury my face in my hands, let the tears flow out of me for the first time since he's gone.

They pour
and pour
and pour
from me.
'Please, Denny . . .

sniff.

Say something . . .

sniff.
I miss you.

Sniff.'

I can barely speak I'm crying so hard.

Something slumps up against the other side of the door.

I freeze.

'I miss you too, kiddo.'

I turn.

Put my cheek against the glass of the door. 'Denny?'

There's a shadow the shape of a hand pressed on the mottled glass. 'Put your hand on mine, Molly.'

'Why? Why can't you just come out?'

'I can't let you see me like this, Molls.'

I put my hand against his shadow. 'I don't care what you look like.'

'Listen – I'm done for. I want you to remember me as I was. Promise me.'

I close my eyes. More tears fall down my cheeks. 'Den, please, *please* just come out. I've found you. Everything can go back to normal now. Everything can be OK again. Just let me in.'

'I said, promise me?' His voice sounds panicky.

I shake my head, not really understanding. 'OK, I promise.'

'You're the most ferocious girl in the world. Don't you never let no one tell you different.'

'Denny, you're scaring me.'

'I love you, T-Rex.'

I push my hand hard against the glass. 'I love you too, tee-oh-oh.'

'Tee-oh-oh.' He laughs. 'Now go, and don't tell anyone I'm here. I don't want you getting in trouble cos of me.'

'But, Den . . .'

'Please, kiddo. This is hard enough.'

I gulp back a thousand tears, get up and leave my brother behind.

CHARGES

I get home.
Ol' Bill are here.
Words hum from their mouths.

Higher charge . . .
Murder . . .
Do you know anything?
If you do and you're
keeping it from us,
you could be in real
big trouble, Molly.

Murder?
Nah.
It can't . . .
it can't be.

The words buzz
round and round.

On my lips.
In my head.
Under my skin.

I have to get Denny
to come home,
he has to tell them.
He's innocent.

THE NOTEPAD

Barely even rubbed the sleep from my eyes, but I need to get word to Denny. This is getting too serious now. He just has to explain to the Old Bill that this is some huge mess up and then he can come home and we can be a family again. If they just speak to him . . . they'll see, they'll *know* he never done it. He would never kill a man. They'll be able to tell that just from looking at him.

There must be something . . . a clue – to bring him home, to prove he's innocent. I need to question him like a proper detective. I need more information and I need it now.

I go round the back of the house on Daster Road, to make sure I don't arouse suspicion, make sure the woman across the road in the car don't see me go in.

I knock on the back door –

tap, tap, tap.

I hope to God he will answer and let me in this time.
There's a rustle from behind the door, but no answer.
'Denny, it's me. Molly.'
'I told you not to come here. You're gonna get yourself in serious trouble. Please.'
'Just open up? I've got something for you.' I pull out his prize possession, his old boxing notepad. I'm hoping it will make him miss home, miss boxing – he must be going out of his mind stuck in this house without boxing. If I can just remind him of what he's missing, maybe he'll come out.

I sit on the doorstep.
Think about the murder charge.
About how I could be done for
knowing where Denny is.
Wonder if I should tell him.

If he's innocent,
why is he trying so hard to hide?
A shiver creeps across my shoulders . . .

I decide ignorance is bliss.
There's no way he'll come out
if he knows they want him for murder.

'I brought you this.' I poke the notepad through the letterbox.
I hear him pick it up.
'Remember your last boxing match?'
Silence.
I begin to tell the story . . .

ROUND 3

My big brother Denny
    Whack
is getting the hell beaten out of him.
    Thud
If he don't sort it out quick,
    Oof
        he's a goner.

The boxing hall is rammed
with blokes –
teeth bared, faces twisted.
Me and Mum are the only girls here.
I don't mind. I sort of like it.

Den takes every punch.
Stands.
    Does nothing.

I get up, lean over the ropes –
    'Come on, Denny. Move it.'
My voice is lost in the manly murmur –
    'Sit down, Molly.' Mum tugs my shirt.
Some bloke bumps into me, spitting beer-
flavoured words into the sweaty air.
    'Finish him!'

I want to knock his block off, but –
ding ding ding – end of round three.

My old man crouches
under the ropes in Denny's corner.
Rubs Denny's swollen cheek,
shouts something.
Denny nods, spits in a bucket,

gets up lively,
    like he's not just taken a beating.

Round four ain't much better.
Denny *jab jab jabs.*
Nothing lands.
The crowd growls.

The other bloke swerves,
catches Denny
crunch   crunch   crunch
Den's cheek *w_obb_les*
across his face.

I wince,
like I've been punched too.
    Denny *slumps* against
        the ropes.
The bloke launches at him –
Whack
face,
crack
chin,
thud
ribs.

Denny's gloves go to his face.
Has he given up?
'Fight back, Denny. Move!'
Mum looks away.
Her heels
tap tap tap
on the ground.
Round five.
Denny smiles at me, cheeky,
winks through his swollen eye.
What's he playing at?
He should be half dead,

but he's messing 'round.

The bloke comes forward,
slower this time, goes for Denny
in his ribs, where he's weak.
    Missed.

Denny laughs, drums his glove on his head.
Showboating. Daring him. 'Try again.'
And then,
like a beast,
Denny unloads –
one, two,
one, two –
a hook here,
body shot there.
Clawing it back,
landing every punch.

The bloke hangs
    on Denny's shoulder,
his eyes roll, gumshield flashes,
the ref   pulls   t h e m   apart.

Denny pulls back,
launches a **solid**
        SHOT

from what feels like a mile away.
The bloke's body melts under him.
No clowning around.
He is
    done for.

We roar, thump our fists in the air
as he goes to the canvas.
What a turnaround, what a bleedin' legend!
That's my brother up there. My Denny.

One.
Den doesn't look at the bloke he's just floored.
Two.
He's chatting to the bookie.
Three.
The bloke's legs t-r_e-m_b-l_e.
Four.
Mum looks up.
Five.
Lets out a sigh.
Six.
Squeezes my hand.
Seven.
I hold my breath.
Eight.
Nine.

He's only gone and won!

The ref pulls Denny's arm in the air.
My brother, the champ.

'That was an epic fight,' he says. 'And you are a boxer – the proof's in your blood.'

'I didn't prove it in my last fight.'

'I heard.'

I wonder how he heard. Frank must have told him. I still want to know what *he* has to do with all this. But right now I have to put that to the back of my mind and concentrate on Denny.

'I really missed you. I've got a fight coming up soon. Be good if you could be there.'

Silence.

'Denny, how did you afford those gloves? Are you mixed up with someone you shouldn't be? Why were you at Duke's that morning?'

'I went in that morning and found him – that bloke, Harry Wilson. It must have happened in the night.'

'Wait? What? He was attacked in the night?'

'He must have been.'

'Then you have an alibi! You were with me. You can come home – I'll just tell them.'

'You're my sister, Molls – they'll never believe it.'

'They will, Den. Please, come back. We can sort this out.'

'I'm getting tired, Molly – you should go.'

I feel powerless.

'Fine, be a coward. You haven't even got the guts to come out and face me. Why don't you stick up for yourself instead of letting your family deal with it all? And why is Frank helping you? Does he know something the rest of us don't? You let him in the other day, but you won't see your own flesh and blood. I know he's helping you. How do you think I found you? I thought you were a fighter, but turns out you're just like the rest of them – a coward!'

I have to catch my breath a minute.

His footsteps move away from the door.

He obviously doesn't like hearing the truth.

Sod him.

Sod this.

I walk away too.

ONE LAST TRY

I wake panicking. Panicking Mum and Dad have guessed I've found Denny.
That the police will come after me. Terrified Denny is never going to forgive
me for what I said.

'Hey, Molly you look tired. Fancy a cuppa?' says Mum.
Why is she saying I look tired?
Does she suspect something?
Is she testing me?

My thoughts are exhausting.
I need to escape.
'Nah, I'm just heading out.'
Mum turns to me, her eyes puffy.
She's been crying.
Again.

An horrific wave of guilt sweeps across me.
I should tell Mum where Denny is.
Let her know he's safe.
Fix her heart.

But I can't.
I've promised Denny –
and you should never break a promise.

He doesn't deserve my loyalty though.
He's being weak, by hiding.
It's as much his fault
as it is Ol' Bill's that we're
all suffering so much.
If he's innocent,
why is he hiding?

Why won't he let me help him?
Maybe he is guilty . . .

Maybe he hurt that man . . . ?

I shake it out my head.
Of course he bloomin' didn't.
This is Denny.

Not some monster.

> My brain buzzes with the hell of it all.
> I grit my teeth.
> Hate myself for thinking it.
> I feel sick.
> Sick.
> Sick of the whole thing.

> I'm going to *drag*
> him the hell
> home if I have to.

He has an alibi,
he was with me.

He fell asleep with that chip in his gob.
I remember it as clear as day
because I took a picture of him—

OH MY GOD!

I took a bleedin' picture of him!

I knock on the door and sit straight down on the step.
'It's me, Denny. Open the hell up.'
A slump on the other side.
'Wish you'd let me in. It's flippin' taters out here. I puff the air and a cloud
of smoke escapes my mouth like I'm smoking a fag.
We sit in silence. I feel his presence even though I can't see him. It feels
good. Even though I'm angry at him, all I want is to hold him and squeeze
him tight.

'Denny, you have to come home. Mum's going out her mind. She never stops crying, and Dad . . . well, even he is going loopy. He spends all day, every day, out looking for you.'

'I can't come home, Molly. Ol' Bill will have me guts for garters. I could go down for life for murder.'

'Oh, you know then?'

'Know what?'

'About the murder charge.'

A pause. 'Yeah, Frank told me.'

It grates on me that he's talking so freely to Frank and not the rest of us. Since when has water been thicker than blood?

I have to know.
To hear it from him.
I take a deep breath,
wish I could look
him in the eyes as I ask,

'Did you do it, Den?'

The longest pause.

I imagine the pain on his face.
I'd do anything to take it back.

'No.' His voice cracks. 'And you wonder why I won't come home! If my own sister has to ask it, what chance do I have with the Ol' Bill?'

'And you're sure that Harry kid was attacked in the night, not the morning?'

'Yeah, I found him.'

I push my hand to the glass of the door. 'I believe you, Denny. I've always believed you. I've got a photo of you at home that night. I took it because you looked so funny with a chip hanging out your gob. We can take it to the Ol' Bill. *It proves your alibi.*'

The door moves
    on my hand.
I look up

and there he is.
Rough stubble
    covers his dimples.
His eyes full of pain.
    He looks a mess.

But
    he's still my Denny.

BUT THEN . . .

a massive thud.
    Denny slams the door.
      Shouting.
        Dogs.
          Scrambling.
        'Get down, get down.'
  I stand up.
    'Denny?'
Shadows is all I can see.
I smash at the door again –

BANG BANG BANG.

      'Den! What's going on?'
    More crashing.
      Smashing.
        Dogs.
    'Get down, get down.'
Denny screaming – 'Run, Molly!'
    I smash at the door.
        'What's going on? Denny! Leave my brother alone.'
          'Run, Molly, run!'
Who's in there?
Thugs? Kidnappers?
I got out my phone, to call the Ol' Bill,
    but Denny told me to run.
I have to get out first, make myself safe.
I leg it to the alley.

The blue.
The flash.
People everywhere.
Ol' Bill – police.
I stop, like I've whacked

straight into a brick wall.

Denny is already outside.

Cuffs.

A police officer each side of him.

No, no, no –

he's innocent!

NO!

'Denny, what's going on? Why are the Ol' Bill here?'

He won't look at me. There's shame in his face. All of his spark gone. The officers lead him to a police car, push the top of his head down, fold him into it, slam the door shut.

I run over. Put my hand on the window. Tears. 'Don't worry – I'll get Dad, Mum too. They'll sort this out. We know you'd never have hurt that bloke, Denny. *We know.* I've got the photo.' He still won't look at me.

I turn to the copper behind me. 'What the hell do you pigs think you're doing with my brother? Let him go! He never done nothing – I have this photo – he's got an alibi – he was with me!' I scramble for my phone in my pocket.

A hand on my shoulder holds me back. The police car drives off. I shove the officer – 'Get your bleedin' hands off me.' I shout after Denny – 'They won't get away with this, Den. Don't worry, Den. Don't worry! We're gonna come get you. I swear it. I'll get you out.'

I turn back to the coppers on Daster Road. 'He's got an alibi – he's got a bleedin' alibi.'

The car disappears round the corner.

My brother is gone again.

'Do you want to get a lift back?' says the policeman. 'It's not good for a young girl to be walking round here. My chief will get you home nice and safe.' He points to a car. Not a police car. A blue car. With a woman wearing normal clothes in the driver's seat.

It's the woman in the car . . .

that I've seen watching me . . .

following me . . .

the *whole* time.

What have I done?

SKILLS

It was the morning of my skills bouts. It wasn't real boxing, just three rounds of controlled boxing to show off what I'd learned, but if I passed, I'd be allowed to box properly.

I could compete.

I was sick as a parrot. My insides was gurgling so much it was like they were having a full-blown conversation with themselves. Saying, *Don't do this. You don't know what you're doing. You're going to fail.*

There was a knock on my bedroom door.

'Yeah, come in.'

'You ready?' Denny whispered.

I looked at him, feeling my lip quivering. 'I dunno.'

'What do you mean, you don't know? No messing now. Can't have Dad finding out what we're up to. Get your kit and let's get out of here. Sharpish.'

I froze. It was like my body was making its own choices and ignoring my brain. 'What if I fail? Then what?'

Denny smiled, stuck his head round the door to check no one was coming and shut it. He put his hands on my shoulders. 'Kiddo, you won't fail. You're a natural.'

'You're just being nice to me.'

'Nah, you've always had a swifty left hook. Do you remember when you were five years old and you clobbered that kid in the sweetshop?'

'What? No. I didn't do that, did I?'

Denny laughed, sitting on my bed. 'Yeah, you did. He looked at your badge and you outright smacked him in the nose. Made his nose bleed and everything. His mother was livid. Was hard explaining that one away.'

'Yeah, but anyone can clobber someone. Boxing's a skill, ain't it?'

'Yeah, but worst thing about that was, when we got home, Mum asked me why you had bruises on your knuckles. Decided right then and there that I was gonna teach you to punch proper, so you didn't hurt yourself and – more importantly – didn't get me in trouble. I remember that first time I showed you. You knew what you were doing. You were fascinated. A real natural. Still are.'

'Really?'

'Yeah, really. So –' he jumped back up to his feet – 'come on. Grab your kit and let's scarper!'

Good old Denny. No matter what,

    he

        never let me down.

PROVING MYSELF

'We're on the undercard.
It's only three rounds,
a minute and a half each.
It's about showing your moves,
about proving yourself.
    Nobody can win.
        It ain't about winning.'
Denny patted me on the back.
    Smiled.

I was against a girl way shorter than me,
her hair in braids, tucked right to her head.
She was mousy, tiny. Bit pathetic really.

Round one, I pounded her.
Knocked her round the ring
like she was a rag doll,
bounce, bounce, bounce.
Show your footwork, Molly!
My ponytail swinging
above my head.

Round two, I pounded her
some more. Enjoyed
the power pushing
from my legs into my arms.
You're a blinkin' legend, Molly!
Like, I can almost see tears in her eyes.
Like, I think she's waiting for me to stop.
Like, I can't see what skills she's showcasing.

Round three, and I wanted
to knock her down and
I know I could,

but Den told me it's not like that.
So I show off all my moves –
show a jab
show a left swing
show an uppercut
show a solid fist in the ribs . . .
she barely moves.

Then it ends.

I go to my corner, duck under the ropes.
'Well done, kiddo!' Den ruffles my hair.
'Bloomin' show-off, ain't you?
You got that one in the bag though.'

And I know,
        even though skills bouts
        aren't about winning,
in Den's eyes, I'd won.

LEFT OUT

It turns out the photo wasn't enough to prove Denny's innocence. The Old Bill used the excuse that he could have woken up after the photo was taken and gone out; nobody saw him leave; and because it looked so shady he went into hiding. It's not looking good for him.

Mum and Dad are off to visit Denny in the nick. But I've got to stay home on my tod, like I'm a family pet or something.

'Prison is no place for a young girl,' says Dad.

'But . . .'

'No buts. For once, do as you're told.'

It's not fair.

I'm the one who found him.

I'm his sister.

He's my blood too.

I need to explain.

I have to apologise.

'There's Spam in the fridge. You make sure you eat something. Got to keep your strength up.' Mum winks at me. She's dressed in her best clothes, wearing a full face of make-up, like she's going to a party or something. She kisses me on my head. Rubs the lipstick mark off, smiles. 'Come on then, let's not keep my baby boy waiting.'

They go.

Both of them.

To see Denny.
Without me.

Cos, as usual,

I don't matter.

THROW IN
THE TOWEL

I'm at Duke's trying to blow off some steam, but even my safe haven feels rubbish now, ever since I found out Frank was hiding Denny and he didn't even tell me. Not even when he saw me in so much pain. I know he was trying to protect him. But I feel let down big time. If he'd let me in on his 'little secret' about Denny, I could have seen him somehow safely, and then I wouldn't have led the Old Bill straight to the blinkin' doorstep.

And now Denny wouldn't be banged up for a crime he never commited.

I look for Kwaku, but he still hasn't reared his ugly face since I was at Flock Heart Rise.

I wrap my wrists, like Denny taught me.

'You all right, Molly?' It's Frank.

'You look tired, Frankie boy – been up all night?' I say teasingly. 'You want to help me with these?' I push out my wrist and chuck the wrap at him.

He catches them and shakes his head. 'It's been a long week.' He looks fed up, the usual sparkle in his eyes missing. I know it's got to be about Denny. I want so much to have it out with him, but I don't want him knowing I followed him to Daster Road.

'You OK, Frank?'

The deep pools of his eyes make my gut swirl. I know how he feels.

He fixes the wrap with the Velcro tight to my wrist. 'Look . . . listen – I know it's not exactly the best timing, but I've just been on the blower about your fight.' He passes me my gloves. I push my hands in. Whack my fists together.

'Awesome!' I say. 'I seriously need to get rid of some anger.'

'Yeah, I heard about Denny. You must be gutted. I never thought he'd do something like that. Murder . . . didn't think he was capable.'

I feel like I'm going to choke. I stare at him dead in the eyes. Make sure he holds my gaze. 'He didn't do it, Frank.'

Frank nods. 'Look, like I said, I've been on the blower, but I need to ask a huge huge favour.'

I grit my teeth. I'm angry at him, but try to keep on a fake chirpy face. He mustn't know I knew his secret about hiding Denny on Daster Road. 'Course, Frank – anything for you.'

He pulls off his cap. 'Thing is, I need you to lose, Molly.'

I pull my wrist back away from him. 'You bleedin' what?'

'I can't explain why, and I know I promised I'd help you win – and I've got faith in you, I really have. But I swear I wouldn't ask if I wasn't desperate.'

'Me losing would affect your reputation as a coach, so I don't get it.' I shove past him. He's obviously winding me up. 'I'll probably lose anyway – I've got a right rubbish coach.' I give him a teasing grin, but his face is serious.

'I really need you to do this, Molly. If this doesn't happen, I'm a goner.'

'A goner? You ain't making sense.'

'I can't say . . . I just need you to trust me.'

I'm tired of people keeping secrets. 'I ain't a baby, you know. If you want me to do something for you, you need to tell me why. I'm fed up of being a mug for people.'

'I'm trying to protect you, Molls. The less you know, the better.'

'Just cos I'm a kid don't mean I can't handle the truth. If you want me to throw my fight, which, if I'm honest, will make me look like a proper melt, then I'm gonna need more info.'

Frank rolled his eyes up to the top of his head, like he was searching in his skull for the right answer, then he let his shoulders slump and leaned in closer, lowered his voice right down. 'I've got these gangsters after me.'

'Rubbish! You're top dog round here. No one would dare come after the legend that is Frank Tessie.'

'They ain't old school, Molly. They don't play by the old rules. These new kids coming in, they don't give a damn about respect or loyalty. All they care about is money and making a name for themselves and this fight you're having.' He paused, anger flooding his face. 'They want to cheat. It's scandalous. Filthy.'

It is filthy. I've worked flippin' hard to get as good as I have. I need to win this fight. Show Denny how good I've got while he's been away. Show him that I never gave up.

'I still don't get it. I'm nobody – I've only had one fight and I lost that.'

'Don't breathe a word to no one, but these East End wide boys are on my turf, taking all my boys, and I'm in debt up to my eyeballs. A lot of my lads have gone off to work for them. They fancy the glamour over the grassroots work. If we don't throw this fight, I'm a dead man. I'll lose Duke's. I'll lose everything. They will make damn sure of it.'

I wonder if Denny is mixed up with these people. *Is that how he bought my gloves? Is that how Harry ended up dead?* 'But why do they care if Janet wins?' I ask.

'They want her going pro in eighteen months and, if she's got a clean record, she'll be more of a pull on the pro circuit. Janet hasn't the foggiest about it, any of it.'

'But she beat me once. Why are they so worried?'

'That's the thing – they weren't bothered. They thought Janet beating you was a dead cert. But they've got eyes, and someone round here has been gassing off about your progress and they reckon it's even stevens now. I ain't saying you'd beat her – she's a tough cookie – but they want a bit of insurance.'

Wow. I feel a twist of smugness. People have heard of me and they think I'm good. I hate the thought of losing. Of cheating. But then again . . . Frank did protect Denny, even though I felt betrayed that he never let me know where Denny was. But at least he tried to keep him safe.

Unlike me.

I suppose I do actually owe him one. 'I'll think about it,' I say.

He puts his hat back on. 'Thanks, Molly.' Then he gives me a little look, that puts a funny feeling in my tummy, and he says, 'I know you won't let me down. You're as loyal as they come.'

He goes back to his office, leaves me training on my tod.

I push it all
aside.
Lose myself in training.
Nobody can get me there.
    Fierce.
        Tight.
        Hungry.
        I've never hit a punchbag so hard.
            Fast.
            Fire.
            Free.
I'm Tyrannosaur.
    I want to
  stamp on the world,
claw the galaxy,
show the universe the real me.

My power.

My   My   My

Roar   Roar   Roar

I run all the way home. Don't waste time waiting for the bus.

Mum's washing up and Dad's watching the telly in the living room. I hide my kit bag under my bed as usual and go and find Mum.

'How was he?'

'He was fine, love. Bit tired-looking. But fine. Why don't you sit down? I'll get you a drink.'

Dad comes in. 'Where you been?'

I clench my teeth. 'Out.'

'Out where?'

'Just hanging about, nothing special.' I turn back to Mum, try to ignore Dad. 'Did Denny mention me?'

'He's got a lot on his plate,' says Dad with a sarcastic smile.

Mum puts a cup of squash in front of me. 'There was a lot to talk about – his case and stuff. Nothing you'll find interesting, love.'

'Did he say why he ran away? As he's innocent, I mean. Why he didn't just come forward.'

'None of your business,' snaps Dad.

'Why not go and watch some telly, love? Take your squash with you. I'll bring you in your dinner when it's ready.'

'I don't want the bloody squash. I ain't a baby.' I push the cup over. It flies across the table and lands on Dad's foot, the orange liquid soaking him. Oh my God, I'm done for.

'Pick that up.'

I stand myself real tall and pull my arms across my chest. 'No.'

Mum picks up the cup, frantically runs a cloth across the floor.

'I ain't messing, Jenny,' says Dad. 'Let her clean up her own mess.'

'Not until you tell me why Denny ran away. I want to help. I can help. Please just let me help.' My lip begins to quiver.

Dad tuts. 'You can't help – don't be stupid, you're just a kid. You need protecting.'

As usual my mouth spills before my brain knows what it's saying. 'I *can* help. Unlike you. It's your fault Den got in trouble. If you hadn't just sat on your arse every day, crying like a baby, and been a better dad, maybe Denny would've had a chance. Maybe we all would.'

'Molly, please, love – can we not do this now?' Mum is making out like I've caused the argument.

Dad shakes his head, tears glaze his eyes. He grabs his paper, looks through it. 'Just leave it alone, Molly – I'm too tired for any of this.' His voice sounds like he's giving up. I should leave it there, but I want to break him. 'At least I tried though. I went looking for him. I found him –' I point to myself – '*me*, this stupid kid right here. *I* found him, not you.'

Dad puts his paper on the table, glares daggers at me. 'Yeah, and look what that led to. If you're so clever, you wouldn't have led the Ol' Bill to him and he wouldn't be in the nick! It's your fault. Maybe he'd be back right here right now, where he belongs.' A tear rolls down his stubbled cheek. Mum gives him a cuddle, like he deserves it. But I don't really care. All I can think of are his words –

Your fault.

My fault.
It echoes, echoes, echoes.
My fault, my fault, my fault.

My head hurts, I feel sick.
I don't want him to be right.
I don't want him to be right.
I don't want . . .

Like a loaded gun, it all shoots out of me. 'You're a rubbish dad! A pathetic failure. You're lazy. You cry like a baby. Hide under your duvet. Denny told me you used to be a somebody, but I don't believe him—'

I don't get a chance to finish. Dad is pulling me to my room. I kick and shout, use all my strength to try to wriggle out of his claws. But it's no use. His strength is mental. I give up and walk the rest of the way myself.

He leads me to my bed, sits me down. 'You stay in here until you learn some respect. I don't want to see your face for the rest of the night. Hear me?' His voice shakes, he's not being mean.

I've got what I wanted.
I've broken him.
So why doesn't it feel good?

I nod.
He turns to leave,
his breath deep and lungy.

He stops.
Doesn't turn round to look at me,
stands still and solid.
His fists flexing.

'I never meant to be a bad dad. I've not been well for a very long time and I'm sorry you've had to pay for that.' The sorrow in his voice swallows the room. I feel myself being sucked into it. Becoming part of it. He leaves without slamming the door.

Not well? In what way?

SPLINTERS

I didn't sleep well last night. Kept waking up thinking of what Dad said. School wasn't much better. Got done about ten times by Mrs Richards for staring off into space. I dunno how teachers expect kids to concentrate on some old, dead poet talking crap, when their lives are falling apart.

I shove the door of Duke's open. It feels heavier than normal cos I just don't have any energy for anything. Everything has pushed me down. I'm spent.

'Hey, Molly, look who's come back.' Tiff is slapping him on the back. It's Kwaku, standing right in the middle of the ring.

I gasp. Anger and happiness. I want to hug him and hit him at the same time. I leg it to the ring. 'Where the hell have you been?'

Kwaku ducks under the ropes, jumps down to me. 'Sorry, I've been busy.'

'Busy? That's all you've got to say? Do you have any idea what I've been through?'

Kwaku doesn't look up, dusts his hands.

'I found Denny. No thanks to you. The Ol' Bill got him – he's in the nick. Could go down for life if we can't prove he's innocent.'

Kwaku throws his towel over his shoulder. 'I heard.'

'So, what we gonna do? How we gonna prove him innocent?'

He ain't his normal Happy Boy self. I know I'm meant to ask if he's OK, but I can't spit the words out. 'I haven't got the brain for this right now. Let's spar.'

We climb into the ring,
put our head gear on,
gumshields in.
Kwaku pushes forwards,
forces me backwards.
    'Easy, mate!'
Whack.

Oof.

Right in my nut.
I fall to the canvas.

Embarrassment.

Then
confusion.

Then
rage.

I throw my gloves off.
Launch myself at him.
        'You bleedin' . . .'
I go for his face,
his ribs.

Even his down-below bits.

He steps back.
Ducks every shot.
        I miss.
        Miss.
        Miss.

His hands go up.
'Woah, woah,
I'm sorry. I'm sorry.'

I lift from the floor,
mitts still punching
the air.
I'm in Tiff's arms.
        'What the hell are yous doing?'

Kwaku's chest beats
        up
        down
        up down
His eyes look sorry.

I slow my breathing.

Rub my head.

Ignore the urge to knock

his block off.

Cos deep down

I know this ain't him.

Something's wrong.

'What's going on with you?'

He takes a gander round.

'Not here.

Let's go somewhere quiet.'

It's funny how many people are walking round with all these worlds inside them. I used to think it was just me who had all this stuff in my head. But I'm starting to see that loads of people are like it. Maybe even everyone. Kwaku's definitely one of them. I reckon he has a bigger world in his head than most people do. That must be hard. I wonder about Dad too, and Denny, and even Mum, and what's going on in their heads, and if it's the same stuff that buzzes through me,

We sit on our bench in the middle of Pear Tree estate. 'Have I done something wrong?' I ask. 'Cos, like, if I did, I'm proper sorry.'

His shoulders stiffen. 'Not everything is about you, you know.'

I pick at the crusty bench. He seems so angry. A splinter digs in under the skin on my thumb. 'I know that. I'm sorry I turned up at Flock Heart Rise. I know someone like me doesn't belong there. I just had a huge lead and I needed you.' I'm relieved to have the splinter, cos it gives me something else to concentrate on.

'What do you mean, someone like you?'

'Cos I'm poor and you live in such a rich place . . . thought maybe you didn't want me shabbing the place up.'

'Molly, life ain't all about money. You can be stinking rich and still be pig miserable.'

'Yeah, but it helps.'

'It might help some stuff, but it can't buy important stuff.'

I push the wood down with the tip of my nail. 'Like what?'

He leans forward, clasps his hands together, dips his head. 'It's my dad. He came back.'

I take my attention away from the splinter, pull my legs up onto the bench. 'But you said he was dead. How could he come back? You been watching too many zombie movies or something?'

He gives me a stinking look. 'It isn't funny.'

I swing my legs back down. 'You're right – sorry. What do you mean, though? Like in a dream or something?'

He shakes his head, does a nervous smile. Long silence. 'I lied, Molly.'

'Lied about what?'

'About him being dead.'

My jaw actually drops. I pull it back in, pretend I'm not as surprised as I feel. 'Who does that? Why would you even—'

He cuts in. 'I was ashamed.' Even by my family's standards, this is pretty messed up. 'That's why I sent you away that day. I was worried you'd see him and find out I'd lied. I thought he might leave again and maybe you'd never find out how much of a nasty liar I am . . .'

Tears well up in his eyes. It makes my heart hurt.

'I'd never think that about you, you daft sod.'

'My mum left him. Years ago. He was in the army. I got called all sorts of names at my old school cos they were divorcing. Dad had an affair with some woman at work. Then he went back to the army and left me too. Didn't hear nothing. He didn't reply to my emails. No phone calls. I really hated him for it. So, when we moved, it was easier to just say he died. When I said that, it stopped people asking more questions, cos they felt awkward. So I told you the same, but now he's back and wants to be my dad again, and my mum says she wants to give it another go. Nobody seems to care much about how I feel.'

I understand that feeing.

'Wow, your family is as much a freak show as mine.'

'Everyone's is, Molly. That's what my mum says anyway.'

'So, you ain't happy he's back?'

'I dunno. Is that bad?'

I shake my head. 'Not everything's black and white,' I say, thinking of Denny.

I pick at my splinter again . . . He fiddles with his hair.

'Are you angry at me?' Kwaku asks finally.

I punch him playfully on the arm. 'No, but next time you've got a confession to make, is it OK if you don't knock me on my ass in front of everyone at

Duke's? I've got a reputation to uphold, don't you know.'

We both smile.

He puts his hand out to me. 'Deal.'

I shake it and nudge him on the shoulder. 'It's nice having you back. I missed that stupid smile of yours.'

'Shall we go back and do some proper training?'

'Yeah – you need to work on that right hook. Barely hurt at all!'

We both laugh.

AND JUST LIKE THAT . . .

I'm tired.
It's been a long day
and I've done a heavy
workout.

I move towards
Duke's exit.
Almost trip . . .
my lace.
Tut.

I lean down.
Do it up.

I get up, to clear
the door –

a heavy mound
bounces
up against
my tiny frame.
    'Oi, watch where you're
    going, you stupid—'

I look up.
A face I've seen
my whole
life long.
My face drops.
One word escapes
my trembling lips –
    'Dad.'

BANNED

from boxing
from Duke's
from picking
up a pair of
boxing gloves

ever again.

END OF MY WORLD

Mum knocks on my bedroom door. God, it's only 7 a.m.! Too early. I just want to sleep the day and the world away.

Mum lets herself in.

I duck under my duvet, peer through a slit between it and the mattress. She puts a plate down on the side. 'You awake, baby?' She sits down on the bed and pulls the duvet away from me. I keep my eyes clamped shut.

Mum flicks my fringe off my cheek and pulls it over my ears. 'I know you're awake,' she says gently.

But I don't give in. I babble, make out like I'm talking in my sleep. Mum says nothing. I'm hoping she'll leave, but she just sits there.

'I made you jammy toast,' she says eventually.

Then, after a few more moments, she pulls the duvet back over me again and sighs. 'He doesn't mean to be that harsh, you know.' She strokes my head. 'He's got his reasons. Things happened that he finds hard to forget. He's got mental health issues – depression. It's not easy for a man to accept that sometimes, but he's getting help. So give it time, yeah?'

I open my eyes just enough to see her face. She looks sad. She looks straight at me. I shut my eyes again, tight. I feel them flickering. Each breath feels heavy, like my breathing's losing its rhythm.

'Anyway . . .' Her voice sounds lighter. She definitely knows I'm awake – we *both* know, but I can't give in now. It'll be too awkward. 'Since you're asleep,' she says, 'I suppose it won't matter if I tell you a little secret. I knew you was boxing the whole time.' She huffs. 'Denny told me.'

I hold in a tiny gasp.

'The silly sod felt guilty about keeping it a secret from his old mum. He said how good you was, and I could see it making you happy, so I never said nothing.'

I jump up from my duvet. 'So it's just Dad who won't let me box then? Why? I'm allowed to have a dream, ain't I? I'm good at it. He doesn't know what the hell he's on about. He might be depressed, but that doesn't give him an excuse to torture me. He's an idiot. I hate him!' and I yank the duvet back over myself, close my eyes, pout.

Mum fiddles with her hands. 'Hate's a strong word, Molly. You need to work on that sharp tongue of yours.'

I don't answer.

She sighs, sits silent for a moment like she's searching for words. Then, 'If you want to be a boxer, find a way to do it. Look how you found Denny. You can do anything –' she pauses, fiddles with her nails – 'but we'd have to find you another gym. Too much history at Duke's. Your dad'll come round. He does believe in you – more than you will ever know – but it's not that black and white. Please try to understand.'

I watch her through the gaps in my lashes. Tears creep through them. She wrinkles her nose and grins. 'It's about your heart and gut. Follow those and you won't ever have any regrets. You can do anything if you put your mind to it.' Mum tugs the duvet right up to my neck, tucks me in tight and kisses me. 'Caterpillar tucksie-insies.'

She gets up. 'Prove Dad wrong. Dreams *can* come true for people like us – we just have to fight for them. It might do Dad good too. Help him forget what happened before you was born.' She goes to the door. 'I know it doesn't feel like it, but he's trying to look after you.'

She leaves the door ajar. I open my eyes, sit up.

Before I was born? What happened before I was born? What does Dad want to forget? And depression, of course. It makes sense now. But how did I miss the signs?

PALOOKA

At breakfast time, Dad sits at the table in the kitchen, head buried in his hands.

'Bit worse for wear, are you?' I put two bits of bread in the toaster and grab the marmalade. He makes a sort of grunting noise, keeps his face buried.

Now is a good time. He's obviously hung over. He'll be weaker in this state than normal.

'Fancy a cuppa?'

He grunts again, nods. 'Two sugars.'

I grab the kettle and turn the tap on. Water splashes all down my top. I wipe it dry with a tea towel. 'Where's Mum?'

'She's out getting me painkillers.'

'Right.' Being his slave, as usual.

'You know it's pointless,' says Dad.

'What is?'

'Sucking up to me – that tea you're making. I'm not stupid. You only offer tea when you want something.'

'I don't . . . I just . . .' I've been rumbled.

'You're not boxing. End of.'

'But, Dad—'

He slams his hand down on the table, sends the ketchup over the side. 'I won't have you in Duke's. It was bad enough when Denny went, but I could never stop him doing anything. With you, it's different.'

'Different? How? Cos you don't think I should dream? You should see me, Dad. I can take on most of the boys in there. I've got a fight coming up – Denny taught me proper good and Frank said—'

'Frank said what?' His face twists. I can hear his teeth grinding. I know he doesn't like Frank – why did I even mention his name?

'Nothing, Dad. It's all right.'

Dad looks sorry. Not a look I'm used to seeing on his face. 'Molly, it's not about you not having the right to dream. Far from it.' He looks as sad as I've ever seen him. Sort of human, soft in the face. Like Mum. I feel guilty for some reason.

'It's OK,' I say, putting a cuppa down in front of him.

Tears glisten in Dad's eyes. It makes me feel queasy. I sit down next to him, put my hand on his back.

'Dad . . . are you all right?'

He shakes his head. 'You're old enough to know the truth. I should have told Denny too, then maybe I wouldn't have lost him. It's time I started fixing things.'

'The truth about what, Dad? What do you need to fix?'

'It's not about dreams, Molly. God knows, I used to be a dreamer myself. Until it happened. It's about you being my little girl and me not wanting you getting hurt. Frank – he took so much from me. It's just about money with him. Never about people.'

I rub his shoulder again. He ain't making no sense. 'Took what, Dad? What did Frank take?'

He leans forward, covers his face with trembling hands. Takes a deep breath.

'It wasn't always this way, you know. I used to be happy. That was before he tricked me. It changed something in my head. Made me bitter. Angry. I've never got it back.'

I slouch back in my chair, hug my tea to my chest and invite the excuses. 'So what did Frank take then?'

He wipes his nose with his sleeve. 'It was before you was born. Denny was only a littl'un himself. Mum was pregnant with you and Frank knew I was desperate for cash. We was pig broke. Your mum, she needed stuff for you; Denny was growing out of his shoes – the money I was earning, it wasn't enough to cover it. Yeah, maybe, if I'd gone and got a nine-to-five, like a lot of them do, I could have brought some extra cash in. But I was a dreamer. I wanted to make a difference. Trouble is, being a good guy doesn't always pay well.'

Dad gets up,
starts pacing,
puts a fag in his mouth,
lights it.

He takes a deep breath
lets out a puff of stinking
smoke, shakes his head.

'That's how Frank did it. Played on my heart. Made out like he was a good guy too. Made out like he could help me. Before I knew it, he had his mitts into me good and proper. Took everything I had away.'

I put my cup down. Shake my head. 'I don't believe you. Frank's a good guy. He's done a lot for me and Denny.'

'Yeah, that's how he got me too. Looked after me good and proper. Then he took it from me.'

'Took what, Dad? What are you on about? You ain't making no sense.'

'Duke's, Molly. He took Duke's.'

'But Duke's is his – what are you even on about? You're just making stuff up to turn me against him. It's wrong. Can't you just let me have this one thing that's good?'

Dad stubs out his fag. 'You're right. I've messed up. I haven't been a very good dad to you.' He crouches down. Puts my hands in his. 'Duke's was mine, Molly, and, before that, it was my dad's. Your granddad's. He built it up from the ground himself. But when I got into money problems, Frank tricked me into signing everything over to him.'

'Why has no one ever said anything about it then?'

'Cos it broke my heart every day. I never wanted anyone to talk about it. Talking about it only made it feel more real. So I made your mother keep it to herself. Denny was too young to know any different. It became something we never talked about.'

'How did he trick you then?'

'He said he was willing to make an investment in Duke's. Enough money to do the place up good and proper, plus tide me over for everything I needed for my family. It sounded great. All he wanted was ten per cent of the business. It sounded well worth it. He was a businessman, after all, and I was never good at that side of things. So I signed a contract and, within the week, there was money in the bank.'

'Sounds like he did you a proper solid.'

'Everything was great. I was walking on air. Anything and everything that you, Denny or Mum needed – it was there. I had nothing to worry about. And not just that – I invested money in Duke's too, which meant I could help more kiddies get themselves off the streets, doing something they felt good about, and that was good for the estates.'

'I still don't understand how all that makes Frank the bad guy then.'

'I ain't an educated man, Molly, and Frank obviously reckoned on that. I never asked a lawyer to look over the contract. But there was a clause in there that said if I didn't make the money back in the first year, then Frank had the right to take over the whole business. The thing is – during that first year, we could have made all that money back easy. But Frank sabotaged it. He spread rumours about the gym, told people I was a wrongun, said I was making shady deals and bets – said I was horrible to the kids in there . . . Before I knew it, the place was dead. Night after night – no one came. I couldn't understand how it had happened at first. But one day, at the end of that first year, Frank came clean. Told me Duke's was his and sent me packing. And when that happened, I didn't just lose Duke's, I lost my livelihood and my reputation all in one snap moment too.'

Frank is a criminal.
    Dad is the victim.
        Everything is upside down.

And for the first time in my life
    I want to cuddle my dad.

He pulls my chin round to make sure I look him dead in the eyes. 'So you see, Molly? I can't let you go back there. I'll take you to another club. But not Duke's. Not with Frank there. He's already taken too much from this family – I won't let him take you too. I'm sorry, baby girl, but I can't risk history repeating itself.'

Mum appears at the kitchen door, tears in her eyes, smudges of black make-up down her face. She's obviously been listening. 'Oh, Rory.' She drops her shopping bags on the floor, pulls him close and wraps her arms round him.

Dad begins to cry.

'It's all right, love, it's all right. At least Molly knows now.'

Mum gestures her hand
    for me to come over.
So I do.
I cuddle
    my mum and my dad
tight
    and the three of us cry,
letting our tears flow.
        Together.

A FIGHT

Denny was looking dead chuffed. 'What's got you all excited?' I whacked the punchbag at him.

'I've got some news, ain't I?'

'Yeah, what's that?'

Frank came out of his office and leaned against the wall, gave us a dodgy look. Denny looked at him, nodded. 'Got Molly her first fight, ain't I, Frankie?'

'Shut up!' I whacked Denny right in the arm.

'Hey, watch it!'

I was so happy. 'You really think I'm ready?'

Denny looked back at Frank, who was pouting like a baby that had lost its dummy. Denny leaned down. 'Course I do, kiddo. You've done four skills bouts now and you've blitzed every one of them. You're going to ace it.'

'Denny,' said Frank, 'my office, now.'

'Do some sparring with Kwaku when he's done changing. Back in a sec.' And with that Denny nipped off, leaving me on my tod.

I grabbed a skipping rope.

I started bouncing –
    clip, flick
    clip, flick.
    Up
    and   over.

My ponytail
    swayed –
    swish, swoosh.
    Up
    and   over.

    Clip, flick.
    Clip, flick.

When Kwaku turned up, we had a solid session on the punchbags. Kwaku corrected my footwork a few times, which bugged me, so I corrected him on his jab – even though there was nothing wrong with it. We kept at it until we were both out of breath.

'Frank said you've got your first fight on the cards. How you feeling?'

It felt weird to know that Frank was talking about me. 'I dunno. I just want to make Denny proud, don't I?' I whacked the bag, let the force of its weight push back at me.

'Ha! Joking, aren't you? That guy would be proud of you if you had three eyes and spoke like a chicken.'

'What does that even mean?' I stopped whacking the bag, steadying it with my whole-body weight so that it didn't knock me over. The bags were proper heavy.

Kwaku pushed at the bag. 'It means, you're like the apple of his eye, aren't you? Before you started coming to Duke's, you were all he talked about.'

Denny talked about me? I thought I was the one who showed off about him.

'Well, we do have a special relationship, I suppose.' I shrugged, like it meant nothing, but I could barely keep the smile off my mug.

Kwaku pulled his arms round the boxing bag so he was hugging it, pulled his feet off the floor, let the bag swing him back and forth. 'You looking forward to his fight?'

I sat down on the floor, crossed my legs, glugged some water from my bottle.

Kwaku jumped off the punchbag, went hurtling to the floor, then sat down in front of me. 'It's all anyone round here can talk about.'

'Bleedin' right an' all. Denny's a legend.'

'Damn straight he is. Man's a warrior. Everyone loves him, especially Frank.'

I loved hearing that. My brother – a legend, a warrior, loved by all.

Kwaku drummed his boxing gloves on the floor, started to make a bit of a beat. 'Do you reckon he'll win?'

Dun, dun, dun, dun.

'He won't just win –' I whacked his glove with a solid thump of my fist – 'he'll obliterate the other guy. He always does.'

'Except last time. That was a bit of a close shave, right?' He drummed the gloves some more.

Dun, dun, dun, dun.
Dur, dur, dur, dur.

'Yeah, well, that was Dad's fault. Things are different now Frank's taken on Denny. Denny says Frank proper looks after him.'

Kwaku smiled. 'Frank reckons Denny could make it semi-pro, the way he's going.'

Dun, dun, dun, dun, dun.
Dur, dur, dur, dur, dur.

I loved how much Kwaku admired Denny. 'Too right he will.'

'First time Frank's had a champ for more than five years.' He drummed the gloves proper hard –

'Yo, Dino Den,
killer of men.
Man's gonna beat you
again and again.'

I cracked up. It was a lame poem, but it was funny.

'Wow, careful – you almost laughed your smile off your face then. It's almost like you're – what's the word? Happy?'

He was a sarcastic git, but he was right. I'd found my place. Duke's and everyone in it had become part of me.

CONFUSION

Kwaku and I are on our usual bench on my estate. I've just filled him in about how Frank ruined Dad's life and stole Duke's from him.

'I've just sort of got this itching in my head. I keep going over the whole Frank thing, wondering if it's connected to any of the clues we found. Like, we never actually found out how Denny afforded those gloves . . . and there's no way he hurt anyone. I know it from the bottom of my beating heart. Denny wouldn't do that. I can't believe the photo for his alibi didn't work – I just don't know what to do.'

'Yeah, and don't forget that Seffi girl and her baby.'

I pull my legs up onto the bench and sit cross-legged. 'Exactly. I mean, why was she so scared? Do you think she meant Frank when she said it's all under our noses? I mean, I thought he was helping Denny when he went to see him – you know, giving him food or whatever – but maybe there was more to it.'

Kwaku scuffs the pavement with his foot, leans down, picks up a stone and chucks it. 'Still shocks me, thinking about Frank being a bad egg. I'm gutted.'

I sigh. 'Yeah. It actually kinda hurts.'

I think back to Mum and Dad arguing, and how Denny had promised things would get better. That was around the time Denny dumped Dad for Frank. When Denny started to change. When he got angry. Missed my blimmin' fight.

Disappeared . . .

My mind flicks back to the photo that Seffi showed me – that little baby, her saying Denny was her man. The question I can't escape, no matter how hard I try, *Is that baby Den's?* I've always been sure he would've told me. But now I know Denny kept secrets. Lies are a big thing for adults. I've been doing my own share of lying lately too. Maybe we all have.

And why does Frank want me to throw the fight? Is he just using me, like he used Dad?

It all spin–

      spin–

            spins round in my head.

Little Bo comes rushing down the path on his trike, his big sister riding behind him. Bo comes to a screeching stop and falls off with a thud. His sister literally throws herself off her own bike, not caring if she gets hurt, just wanting to get to him. Protect him. 'Here,' she says, rubbing his knee, 'magic dust will make you feel better.'

I smile.

It reminds me of when I was little and Denny used to do that kind of stuff for me. He never cared if he got hurt or in trouble – protecting me, that was his number-one priority. And just as when I was too young to protect myself *he* did it for me, now he finds himself too vulnerable to protect himself then *I* have to do it for him.

'I need to get to Denny,' I say. 'But I'm not allowed to go see him. I think we need Seffi.'

'Joking, ain't ya? She made it pretty clear she don't want nothing to do with any of it – and that was before the murder charge.'

'I've got to try.'

I pull out my phone.

Seffi, we need your help

SUSPICIONS

Seffi is chain-smoking,
black marks under her eyes.
It's obvious she's been crying.

I've been to see him.
Like you asked.
He wasn't happy about it.
I wasn't happy about it.
But I never gave him much choice.
Like you didn't with me –
all that guilt-tripping.

Anyway,
he's told me something.

She's shaking her head,
like something is
eating away at her.

You should have seen him.
Broke my little old heart.
He's lost all his swagger.
Lost weight too.
Can't imagine what they're
feeding him in there.

She lights another fag.

Look, I dunno what to say
to yous to be honest.
It ain't looking too good.
I dunno how he's gonna
get out of this one.

I wish she'd just get on with it.
I know you think he's innocent –

Damn straight I do.

– but it's just . . .
Well . . .
Molly,
there's a witness.
Says he saw him
do the whole thing.

Someone's been
a bleedin' grass.
And – worse – a liar.

It makes you wonder.
I mean, maybe . . . I dunno . . .
these things happen,
don't they?
Even good people –
they do stuff that's wrong
sometimes.

You see it in the news all
the time.
People like us,
we're fighting for
our lives out here.

She thinks he did it.

Anyways, I don't know
what else to tell yous.

She gets up,
stubs her fag out.

Good luck.
I gotta think
of my boy now.
This ain't healthy for him.
Much as it breaks my heart.
I've already done more
than I said I would.

I have to ask –
'Is the baby Denny's?'

Tears in her eyes.
She wipes her wet cheek.

What? Hayden?

She smiles.

No.
His blood dad's long gone.
But Den is smitten.
Wanted us to be a
proper family.
Blended.

He says blood don't matter
and he loves Hayden,
like he's his own.

He wanted to introduce
us to yous,
but he wanted to get your
fight out the way first.

Didn't want to drown
your spotlight.

My heart is beating out of my chest.
Relief.
I knew he wouldn't have
hidden *that* from me.
Just like I know he's innocent.

I need to find out who this witness is.
Before it's too late.

GRASS

I smash through Duke's doors,
run to Frank's office.
He's not there.

I stomp out,
look round the room,
every face I used to trust
is now a suspect.

'Which one of yous done it?
Which one of yous is a grass?'

My shout echoes round the hall.
Everyone stops what they're doing.
Blank stares.

Confusion on faces
as they look at each other,
wondering.

Wondering what's got into
this crazy girl.
'Well?' I say.
'Didn't you hear me?
Which one of yous
is a dirty rotten grass?'
No one comes forward.
But then I spot it – the look on her face.
Guilt. Shame. Humiliation.

'Tiff?' I say.

She pulls off her gloves,
seems to look across

at Frank's office,
like she's scared of something.

'I'm sorry, Molly.
I had no choice.'

I LIKE TO BOOGIE

Kwaku and I are out of breath from running to my gaff.

We bash through my front door and into my bedroom. I grab my T-Rex gloves from the cupboard and shove my mitts into them.

'What's with the gloves?' he asks.

'Just trust me.'

I pull Kwaku into the living room. Mum and Dad are cuddled up on the settee watching telly.

'Dad, I know what happened to Denny. Frank set him up.'

'What're you on about?' says Mum.

'Yeah, what's going on?' says Dad. 'Sit down a minute. You look white as a sheet.' He pats the settee next to him.

'No, I won't!' I stand tall, my shoulders back, put my fists up and start pouncing about the living room.

'Who's this?' asks Dad, eyeing Happy Boy.

Kwaku puts his hand out to shake Dad's, like a right melt. 'Hey, I'm Kwaku. Pleased to meet you, Mr Levine.'

Dad doesn't take his hand, just sort of looks at him, like he's an alien from out of space.

I grit my teeth and it all comes spilling out. 'I won't sit down. I won't shut up. I'm not a baby no more, and it's about time you listened to me. Denny bought me these gloves.' I hold my hands up. 'Three hundred quid they cost him.'

Mum and Dad's faces are pure shock. Dad turns off the telly.

Now I have their attention.

I get into my best boxing stance and leap about on my toes, mitts up, ready for a fight, ready to win.

Dancing!

One, two.

Jab, jab.

I pretend to punch Kwaku in the chest, then spring my fists back up for defence. 'Denny's got this new girlfriend and she's got a baby.' Deep breaths escape me.

It's like an exorcism, telling the truth –

huh,

huh,

huh –

More shadow punches. This time I direct them at Dad.

'You what?' says Mum. She chucks her magazine on the floor and stands up square to me. 'What do you mean, Dennis has a girlfriend with a baby? He never said. He would have said. Ain't that right, Rory? He would have blinkin' said.' Her voice comes out all raspy, like she's out of breath. She holds her chest, falls back onto the settee.

Dad does a proper belly chuckle. 'Your mum's right. He would have said. You're acting crazy.'

I *smash* my
gloves together.
One, two,
    one, two.
Left, duck,
    right, duck.
Upper
cut,
    to the side,
    knees in,
    elbows in.
Dancing,
      dancing,
         dancing.

This time my eyes lock with Mum's. Inside the serious shock on her face is a twinkle.

Kwaku gives me his Happy Boy smile. 'She's a tyrannosaur –' he points at me, almost laughs.

I beat my chest with my glove.

'Better watch me roar.'

Kwaku does a little dance.
'Like a matador. Go, girl!'

I bounce some more.
Watch my footwork.
Shadow every boxing

move in the book.

Show them who I am.

My roots, my dreams.

Everything inside me ROARS.

'Denny must have been working for Frank if he could buy these gloves. Reckon Frank got him trusting him good and proper, then he set him up. He's got everyone in his pocket. The witness they got against Denny? It's Tiff from the gym. Frank paid her to do it cos she was so behind on her rent. She needed the money to keep a roof over her kids' heads. He set Denny up, Dad, just like he did to you when he took Duke's off of you.'

He looks up at me. 'Molly, how—'

'So will this Tiff come forward?' says Mum, interrupting him. 'Will she tell them Denny never done it?'

'She won't. She's too scared – and I don't blame her. We have to get Frank another way.'

'I need to go see him,' says Mum.

'No, no way. I ain't having it. It's not happening.' Dad is flustered.

'Tiff says Frank keeps CCTV videos in his office,' I explain. 'If I can get in there, we can get solid proof of who done it and find out who Frank's protecting.'

'It's too dangerous, Molly,' says Dad.

Mum puts her hand on his chest. 'Listen, Rory – it's for Denny. We have to try, and we can be outside, waiting, so nothing will happen to her. It could be our only chance.'

'Or I could go down there and beat two bells out of him.'

'And how is that gonna help Denny?' Mum turns to me. 'Let's do this.'

'There's one more thing—'

'Oh, this just gets better and better,' says Dad.

'You've got to let me fight at Duke's. Frank wants me to throw my fight. He reckons he's done for if I don't. He's got some dangerous men after him. He wants me to lose, but I'm gonna win. Maybe we can't get him sent down for framing Denny, but we can get a different kind of justice.'

'Poetic justice,' says Kwaku, his face beaming.

'Uh, no,' I tut. 'Street justice.'

Mum turns to Dad and crosses her arms, then she looks at me. 'Yes, we will let you fight. Won't we, Rory?'

Dad jumps up. 'Jenny, this is crazy. She's just a kid.'

'Look at her, Rory. I think she's proved herself.'

I punch out again –

huh,

    huh,

        huh.

Dad pinches his nose. 'I can't let that man hurt another one of my own.'

Mum starts poking Dad in the chest. 'So we just let him get away with hurting Denny?' – *poke.* 'Ain't he one of our own?' – *poke.* 'It's about bleedin' time Frank Tessie learned a lesson –' *poke, poke, poke.*

'Look at her, Rory. You know better than anyone – boxing runs in the blood.' Mum puts her hands on my shoulders, starts leading me toward the kitchen. 'Let's hear this plan of yours then, Molly.'

'Wait,' says Dad. He looks more nervous than I ain't ever seen him before. 'If you're fighting, then you'll need a coach.' He grins with his teeth clasped tight, scratches the back of his head, grabs my boxing gloves still on my hands, holds them in his, examines the stitching. 'T-Rex?' He nods. 'That's about right.'

'Denny named me. Like Granddad named him.'

Dad smiles.

'Let me help you win, Molly.

        Let me be your dad again.'

ROPE-A-DOPE

My heart is thumping like a goodun as I open the door to Frank's office.

He jumps up from his desk. 'Molly, just the girl I need to see.'

His fakeness make me go stiff, but I smile, all sweet.

Frank shuts the door and leads me in. 'Have you thought about it?' He pulls out a chair, pats it with a hairy white hand.

He goes to the window, pulls down the blind. I go stiff again. *What if he knows I'm on to him? Is he shutting the blinds so no one can see what he's gonna do to me?*

I try to remember that Mum and Dad are just across the road in the 24-hour café and I've got my phone in my pocket ready to call them if things get dodgy.

I fiddle with my ponytail.

'Have you thought about what I asked?' he asks again.

'Yeah.'

His wrinkles stiffen.

His cracks look black.

For the first time,

I see the real Frank.

The darkness.

His eyes,

swirling pits.

He is empty.

How did I not

see it before?

Right under your noses.

'Well?'

'I'll do it.'

He sits back in his chair. 'That's my girl.'

I dig my nails deep into the palm of my hand until it hurts. I ain't his girl.

I ain't his anything.

I'm not a possession.
I'm *my* own.

He pulls a fag out, taps it on his desk, once, twice, three times, lights it, happy as Larry.

A stupid part of me feels sorry for him. He has no idea what's coming, even though he deserves it.

'You've done so much for me,' I say, 'and, like you said, there'll be plenty more fights to win.'

'Thank God for that! As soon as all this is over, we will get you another fight and make sure you win it.'

We shake on it.

My heart's beating fifty billion miles an hour.

Knock knock –

Right on time.

Tiff's at the door. 'Frank, we need you out here a sec.'
Frank nods. 'Be right back.'

I don't have long.

SHARPISH

I go straight for the
cupboard.
That's where Tiff
said it'd be.

It's full of tat.
It's gonna take me ages . . .

I fiddle and I rummage.
My hands shaking.
Beads of sweat
on my face.

There's nothing here!

I scan the cupboard again.
It's so messy
I can't see for looking.

But then –
What's that?
Something looks
out of place.
At the back.
Is it loose?

I glance towards the door.
He won't be long.

Panic. Panic. Panic.

I yank the corner
of the cupboard.

It comes away from the wall.
Behind it, there's a
gap
that goes down to the floor.

I reach in,
so my body is in the
actual cupboard.

Getting stressed.

This is taking too long –
he's gonna catch me!

My hand fumbles.
The darkness,
dust, dirt,
spiders' webs – *yuck*.

Then . . . something
rectangular . . .

Something falls—
Clunk.

I freeze.
My heart stops.
I wait for Frank
to come barging through
the door.

But nothing happens.

Jammy git – I got away with that.
Quick, I need to be quick!

I pull the object out

and close my eyes,
praying, begging.

Please let it be . . .
I open them.

Thank God.

It's in my hands.
Denny's ticket to
    freedom.

HURRY

'Did you get one?' Mum asks Dad before he's even got halfway through the door.

'Do you know how hard it is, finding a bleedin' video player in this day and age? Lucky Mr Geary had one. He's still stuck in the Dark Ages. Ain't even heard of internet or DVD players.'

'Never mind that, Dad – plug it in.'

We all wait for Dad to set it up.

I can hardly wait a second longer. 'Hurry up, Dad!'

'Give me a bloomin' chance.' He whacks the video player and puts the CCTV tape in. All four of us – me, Mum, Dad and Kwaku – sit on the settee together.

Brace ourselves for the big reveal,
the climax after the cliffhanger – like the
ending of some old whodunnit film . . .
But this is real life.
And I ain't on the edge of my seat in a good way.

Cos somewhere in the back of my mind
I'm absolutely terrified that, when it comes down to it,
    Denny did do it.

THE PREMIERE

We fast-forward,
through empty space.
Bin men collecting bins,
a postman, an Avon lady.

A young guy comes
to the door.
This must be him.
It's not Denny.
I don't recognise him,
but the police could
identify him from this –
the picture is clear.

He's loitering in the alley.

Someone comes up
behind him, towards
the door. He's got a hoodie on.
I can't see his face.
But he's too short to be Denny.
That'll be enough to
prove him innocent, surely?

Now I'm not sure which one's
gonna be the victim.

I start to get sicky,
wondering what I'm gonna see,
how violent it might be.
I hold a cushion against my chest,
ready to hide behind it.

They look like they're arguing,

their arms thrashing the air,
angry gestures.

Then –
BANG –
the hoodie guy
sucker punches the other one.
He lands like a deadweight on the floor.
I clutch the pillow tight.

Hoodie guy
prods the body with his foot.
But deadweight guy is sparko.

Hoodie guy gets his phone out,
pulls back his hood –

but he's facing the other way,
as if about to make his escape . . .

Why's he hanging around?
I'd scarper if I was him.

He puts his phone back
in his pocket,
reaches in the other –
it looks like he's got
keys or something,

he turns round –
and I recognise him
right away.

        It's Frank.

Dad stops the tape.

HAND IT OVER

I'm at the police station.
Clutched in my hands –
the CCTV tape.
We hand it over.
Expect them to hand
Denny over in return.
But they say it will
take some time.

It'll be worth the wait.

MOLLY MONTAGE

'Ladies and gentlemen, may I present Happy Boy K on the mic . . .'
    Kwaku steps forward. I plonk myself down on the settee with Mum and Dad.

Yo, she's all good.
Drum roll
please.
Molly 'Tyrannosaur' Levine.
Yeah. Yeah. Yeah.
Ready!

Main girl Molly doing some running,
skipping, hill sprinting. Girl's been gunning.
Don't underestimate her cos she's cunning –
fists like that she's gonna be stunning.
Now she's doing press-ups with her old man.
He's giving ribs 'bout her attention span.
Chair sit-ups, clap push-ups – girl's got a plan –
moaning so much, better call her Tarzan.

Speed bagwork – watch her go fast.
Footwork drills – she ain't no outcast.
Heavy bag – she'll put man in a plaster cast –
girl's gonna win, yeah, that's the forecast.

Watch her sparring in the ring – girl is high spec.
Getting hit, so many times, gives her respects.
Mirrors, shadow boxing, taking subjects –
don't call her king, call her queen: she's a T-Rex.
Shouted at by her dad cos she's lazy,
giving up cos she's tired and she's shaky.
Looks at a pic of her bro . . . makes her hazy –
she pushes harder, punching gloves. Girl be gravy.
Kisses gloves Denny got her, gold stitching.

Gonna be queen of the ring, yeah, winning .
Beat Frank to the floor with her witching –
this girl's ready to win. She be itching.

   Bam!

We all three clap, cos it's brilliant.
'What a wordsmith,' Mum says.
'That's a real talent you've got there, son,' agrees Dad.

And me? I just smile.

ALWAYS TOGETHER

I know now more than ever,
    I have to win.
    We have to win.
    All of us.
    Inside of me is
    everything.
    Everyone.

The good, the bad,
the worst of all the things
that have ever happened to me,
the best too.

All smushed in.
All the training.
All the failures.
All the nice things.
All the proper nasty stuff.
And all of it is
    OK.

Even the bad stuff,
the stuff I've done wrong,
the stuff I am ashamed of.
It is all in my roar.
All of it.
Denny might not be here,
but it's
    OK.
                Together, the rest of us will fix it.

Denny is always with me. I don't need him here to feel his presence. Can't get rid of the bugger even if I wanted to. But I do have Kwaku, Mum and Dad,

Tiff, Seffi and Hayden by my side.

> I can win.
> But *I*'m the one who can do it.
> It's only me
> that can stand
> in the ring.
> Only *I* can fight.
> Only *I* can try.
> Only *I* can win.

But all winners need help,

> and for the first time in my life
> I have a *team.*
> And I can tell you for
> nothing –
> I am bleedin' ready.

FIRST MEMORIES

I was five years old
and my big brother,
my hero,
was teaching
me to punch.

I had gloves on
that were so big
they nearly toppled
me over.

'Punch like this,
with a straight wrist.'

He tapped my tiny arm.
I scrunched my nose up,
and with all my might
I punched him in his belly.

He clapped, pretended to fall back.
'That's it, kiddo!
You've got it.
One day, you'll be
a champion.'

ON THE ROPES

Kwaku's wrapping my wrists. He has to be careful, cos I twisted it during training the day before yesterday and it's weak.

Just my luck.

Mum's putting my hair in a braid. Dad's in the hall. We can't risk Frank seeing him, but there was no way he was missing my fight, so he's hiding out, wearing a tatty baseball cap . . . looking shady as hell. He'd be less suspicious if he'd come dressed normally.

'Remember what your dad told you about keeping your right hand protected.'

I nod. 'I'll be fine.' I'm putting on a face, but deep down I'm worried about it.

Frank comes into the changing room.

'What's she doing here?' He looks at Mum with suspicious eyes. I know it was stupid having her here, but she'd said there was no way she'd leave me with 'that scumbag'. Mum can be blinkin' scary sometimes and I wasn't going to argue with her in that mood.

Mum turns to Frank. Puts her hands on her hips, looking crazy confident. 'I'm here to watch her win.'

'Yeah, she's got a right little crowd of us,' says Kwaku. 'Seffi's here too.'

'Rory here?' asks Frank. The colour drains from his face.

Mum looks at him, barely hiding her scorn. 'Don't be daft. You know he won't set foot in here again.'

Frank ignores this. 'Right, well, both of you, out. I want a word with my fighter before she fights.'

Mum looks worried, but I ain't scared of him. 'It's OK, Mum. See you out there.'

She nods. 'Come on, Kwaku, let's get some good seats.'

Frank turns to me. 'What the hell is she doing here? If she gets wind of our plan—'

'Relax! She's got no idea. She found out I was boxing and got all excited about watching me. It would've been more suspicious if I'd said no. You know what she's like.'

Frank nods and his mind seems to drift off somewhere. 'Right,' he says after a moment, 'fine. If you say so. You ready for this?'

'Course. A deal's a deal, ain't it? I won't let you down.'

'Good . . .' He pauses, looks at me like his whole life depends on this fight. 'Do it for me too. You know how much I've invested in you. There's a lot to be lost if this goes pear shaped. But, lucky for us, bookies have it that Janet's favourite to win. So you might not have to fake anything, eh?'

I nod, a bit annoyed the odds are against me.

'That's my girl.' He ruffles my hair, kisses his hand and slaps it on my cheek. 'You're one of the most loyal kids I've had in here, you know that? Like the daughter I never had.'

And in that moment, I honestly think he believes what he is saying.

MOLLY 'T-REX' LEVINE VS JANET 'HAWK-EYE' HASSAN – THE REMATCH

PRE-BOUT

Rap music. Hands in my gloves. One weak, one strong. Crowds cheering. Feet firm. The swing in my hips, steady. People shout my name. Elbows lock. I am focused. Breath steady. Ready to fight. Ready to win.

'You can do this,' says Kwaku.

I nod.

Mum ties my hair tighter. Right off my face. No chance of it getting in the way. She smiles. Kisses me on the head. Whispers, 'Proud of you.'

Frank pushes my mouthguard in. I try not to wince. He taps me on the side of the head, puts my headguard on.

I bend down, put my foot on the canvas and wink at Kwaku.

'You just do your best, that's all you can do. Whatever happens – I'm proud of you,' says Mum.

Frank gives me a testing stare. Like he might know what's going on. Then he sits on the side.

I look for Dad . . . he's at the back. He gives me a thumbs up. Seffi's sitting a couple of rows back from the ring, bouncing Hayden on her knee. Tiff next to her. Mum and Kwaku ringside, with Frank looking annoyed. I kiss the stitching on my gloves. T-Rex. 'This one's for you, Den.'

They are all *here*.

Janet stares across the canvas at me.
She looks less scary than last time,
but her eyes are still angry.
I swing my head side to side,
warm my muscles.
My eyes lock with hers.
She pushes her mouthguard in.

Points.
Thumps her chest.
I know what that means –
she wants to kill me.
But there's no chance
I'm gonna lose this time.
Even if my life depended on it.

Ding ding ding!

ROUND 1

We dance
first one way
then the other
up
hands up
elbows *in*

the squeak
of trainers
as we
s
p
i
n

my eyes lock with hers . . . until
B=A=M
she goes right for my chin
and
crack –
I $w^ob{}_b{}^je$
but
it doesn't
hurt.

I sneer.

Her eyes pure fury, she comes in, again –

miss

again

miss

I crack back

      right in her ribs

            take the wind out of her

               oooof

                  she e-x-h-a-l-e-s **hard**

                 I almost *fall over*

               like a sail in the wind.

'Get her.' Kwaku.

I go for her left side,

      miss

            then *jab, jab, jab, jab, jab, jab*

    one

        side

          then

            the

               next

      jab, jab, jab, jab, jab, jab, jab, jab, jab.

            I STOP

            to recover

and she comes in with an uppercut from nowhere.

          Ouch!

        That one hurt.

Ding ding ding!

CORNER

Frank: *[mopping my brow]* That's my girl. You was doing a blinding job up there. Be careful though. Don't get too tired. Got a bit overworked at the end and she caught you. It only takes one of them and it don't matter how many you give, she's got you on a knockout. *[Winks. In a whisper]* You're doing a good job. Keep up the act.

Kwaku: Mate, remember: Float like a butterfly, sting like a bee. *[Smiles broadly.]*

Me: *[taking deep breaths – puff, puff, puff]* Mind and body.

Frank: *[Gives another knowing wink.]*

Ding ding ding!

ROUND 2

Back in we go. Back into the lair. She's watching. But this time she looks muddled.

      Like, she knows I've got this

           I am going to win.

We do the dance. I wait . . .

      float

         float

            float.

She waits too. But I'm better at it. I've been doing a lot of waiting lately.

      She gives in.

      A solid jab, right in my ear.

      I feel it

      ringing

      buzzing

      muffled.

      I squint my eyes tight,

      push my teeth together,

      ringing

      buzzing

      yeeesh.

      She comes in again for the other side –

      I duck.

      Still the ringing.

      She goes for the ribs –

I skip, skip, skip.

Let her get tired.
She's angry – let her anger take over. She's not thinking.
This is what I want.
She tries and tries. I duck, swerve, dive, skip, dip,
then I tap my head with my fist –
'Come on, you can do better than that.'
She

lunges

forward,
like Rocky Balboa,
the Italian stallion himself.
But I whack her right in the chin
and she

top-

top-

topples.
almost

almost

almost

losing her
balance.
The crowd go mental.
Bet they ain't seen nothing this exciting for time and a half.
I breathe, take it all in
and she . . . hits . . . me . . . right . . . in . . . the . . . gut –

I retaliate
with
the
wrong hand.
I feel it *crunch.*
Dazzled, I stumble on the ropes.
All I can feel is the pain
in my wrist.
It creeps into my belly.
I want to be sick.

She lays into me –
one, two, one, two.
Each hit lands like a truck ramming into me.
Thank God the bell goes –

Ding ding ding! –

cos my legs almost go from under me.

CORNER

Frank All right, all right. *[Shoving a drink in my mouth]* Have a drink.
Kwaku – brow. Now!
Kwaku: *[Mops my brow.]*
Frank Look, you can't get cocky like that. Not when you've got an injury. You've
gotta keep it back. Protect it. *[More stupid winking.]*
Me: *[Spinny head getting better]* I thought I had her.
Frank: You got carried away and forgot to use your brain. You're still ahead on
points. But only just. Sort it out. Stay focused. *[i.e. Lose.]*
Kwaku: Yeah, look, you're in the final round. You're already more ahead than
last time. You can win this. I know it. Put your hand behind you if you have to.
Molly: *I can do it. I can do it. I can . . . do . . . it. Can't I?*

Ding ding ding!

ROUND 3

I get up,
bit wobbly
head a bit
wooooooh,

> and that gut thing,
> that I can win this thing –
> it's sort of gone
> and I'm digging around
> trying to find it. Where is
> it? Roar, *roar . . . rrrraaaa . . .* bleurgh.
> I can't beat her with one hand.

She's moving forward,
coming for the kill.
Who am I kidding?
Of course I can't win.

        She ducks in for a jab –
        s—w—e—r—v—e

I pull my right hand behind my back,
to stop me from using it, stop
her from getting at it.

        I hit back, just a skim on her chin –
        Head too fuzzy, tummy too sicky,
        legs too wobbly . . . I hold on to her.

She whacks me.
in the ribs – *Ooooooooof* –
I hit back, miss.

She pushes me up against the ropes
        – I try to get out of her clutches
        but the fire in her eyes is back.
        I can't let her win – I can't let Frank win.
        I try again, *roar, raaaah, rahhhh*—
        choke, splutter. Like a car engine
        that refuses to start. I can't find my starter
        motor. I take punch after punch after . . .

'Don't you dare,'
        comes a voice from the side.

'The Molly I know doesn't give up.
She's a bleedin' pain in my ass
cos she never ever gives up.'

It can't be . . .
    I duck round Janet to have a look. But she ain't giving in. I push her.

Energy from nowhere.

Roooaaaaar!

She stumbles, but lunges back at me.

'Get out my way!' I punch her right in the cheek *crunch*. Dance my way around . . .

'That's it, girl! T-Rex Tyrannosaur! Go, southpaw!'

It's him.

It's really him.

It's Denny.

Kwaku joins in,

'Ty-rann-o-saur, Ty-rann-o-saur, Ty-rann-o-saur!'

Then Mum, then Seffi, Tiff . . . and I'm sure I can hear Dad at the back too.

'Ty-rann-o-saur!'

Then the crowd joins in too –

Ty-rann-o-saur,
Ty-rann-o-saur,
Ty-rann-o-saur!

I don't believe my eyes . . .
my ears . . .
Janet is back up in my face.
I spin round, crack her in the ribs –
Denny is here to see me –
whack her on the chin,
thud in her ear.
I release all my anger, all my pain, into her.
Into *my* fight.

She's huffing, puffing, wobbling.
Everything in me is unloading.
Unravelling.

But in a clever way.
A focused way.
Bam, bam, bam.
I am T-Rex!
I am dinosaur.

CRUNCH

Crunch

Crunch

crunch

ROAR   ROAR   ROAR

tearing,

ripping,

growling

her out of existence.

One last crack, southpaw.

Molly Levine – Tyrannosaur.

Roar   ROAR   **ROAR!**

STOP, STOP, STOP

Everything goes echoey. It's like I'm watching my own life happening. The ref is waving, pulling us apart. Judges whispering. She falls to the canvas. Doesn't get up. The ref is counting.

I stumble across the canvas.

It's over.
They're saying I've won.
Knockout!

I duck under the ropes.

They're saying we gave the boys a run for their money. They can't wait to make money out of us.

I leap right into him.

I hear it, I know what they're saying.
They're saying I'm a champion.
But I don't care,
      cos I'm holding my big brother tighter than I've held anything in my whole life long and I never want to let him go, ever again.

BELOW THE BELT

Over Denny's shoulder, I see Frank duck under the ropes and march towards us. His face pure rage.

Crimson red.

'Den, it's—' I try to warn him, but Frank already has hold of Denny's shoulder. 'How the hell did you get out the nick?' He looks all round him, paranoid.

Denny pulls me behind him, squares up to Frank. Dad jumps in the middle of them, puts his hand on Denny's chest. 'It's not worth it, son. We've beaten him. It's done.'

Denny pushes at Dad for a second, then puts his hands up in the air and steps back.

Frank's face drains. 'Rory . . .'

Dad ruffles my hair. 'Came to watch my girl win, didn't I? Glad the training we gave her paid off.' He looks around. They are all in the ring with me – Mum, Kwaku, Seffi . . . even Tiff has appeared too. She smiles at me, gives a thumbs up.

Frank is outnumbered.

'Molly, can I have a word please?' he says.

I keep my eyes fixed firmly on the canvas.

'She ain't going nowhere,' says Denny.

'She's *my* fighter.' Frank looks at Denny like he's stupid. 'Come on, Molly. It'll only take a minute.' He puts his hand on my shoulder.

'I don't want to,' I croak.

Seffi yanks his hand off me, folds her arms across her chest and blocks his way. 'She said no.' She looks proper tough. Even with all my boxing moves, I wouldn't start on her.

Kwaku stands in front of me too. 'Yeah. She said no.'

Then Mum, Dad, Tiff and, finally, Denny – all of them are round me, like a wall, guarding me from Frank.

'We had a deal, Molly.'

'What, a deal to stitch her up?' says Kwaku.

Frank doesn't take his eyes off me. 'I dunno what she's told you lot, but all I've done is help her, ever since the first day she came to Duke's. I took you in as one of my own, Molly, and this is how you repay me. I helped you too, Denny. When the police was after you, I hid you, didn't I?'

Denny pipes up. 'Oh, do me a favour. You ain't no victim. You're a wrongun through and through. You set me up, just like you did to Dad all those years ago.'

'I didn't hear you complaining when I was training you to go pro.'

'Then you fed me to the lions.'

'I treated you as my own.' Poor Frank, I could almost feel sorry for him. He has no idea that we know he was the one who assaulted Harry.

Seffi pushes forward and slaps Frank right in his ugly mug. 'You set my Denny up.' Then she whacks him in his chest over and over. Frank just looks down at her.

'I dunno what you're on about. Hey, Den, get your missus off me.'

Denny pulls Seffi back. 'Leave him, love. He ain't worth it.'

Frank's face twists with fury, then changes to sheer desperation. 'I never done nothing.'

Kwaku stands forward, right next to me, my partner in crime. 'We've seen it, though. Molly got the CCTV tape you had hidden in your office.'

Frank looks at me. 'How did you get your mitts on that?'

Dad smiles, huddles me into him. 'Turns out you ain't the only one who can pull the wool over people's eyes.'

Frank turns on me. 'Grass!'

'If saving my brother makes me a grass, I'd do it again and again.'

Frank covers his face in his hands. He pulls off his hat, ruffles his hair, then puts his hat back on. He turns to face Dad, with the longest, saddest stare I've ever seen. Then, eventually, he nods. 'Gah, to hell with you all!'

He turns, grabs his coat and boxing gloves, which he clutches to his chest, then looks round Duke's one last time.

Just as he reaches the door, a man and woman dressed in smart gear come in.

'Are you Frank Tessie?' says the woman.

'Who's asking?' says Frank, buttoning up his coat.

'I'm Detective Inspector Morgan, and this is my colleague, Detective Inspector Oyoye.'

Frank bolts.
DI Oyoye wrestles him
to the ground.
Frank is
    screaming – 'Get your filthy pig hands off me!'

They pull him to his feet.

I stand forward, smile, nod,
    'I did what I had to do to protect my own.
    You wouldn't understand, Frank. It's called loyalty.'

My words are like daggers to him.
He almost loses his balance.
But then, after a short pause,
he holds out his hands for the cuffs.
    'Take me.
    I'm probably safer in the nick anyway.'
They pull his arms
behind his back.

The woman detective is saying,
    'Frank Tessie,
    I'm arresting you on suspicion of murder.
    You do not have to say anything.
    But it may harm your defence
    if you do not mention when questioned
    something which you later rely on in court.
    Anything you do say may be given in evidence.'

They pull him towards the door.
He looks back, winks, says,
    'Be lucky,'
then off they take him.

He's gone.

Frank Tessie
is no more.
It's over
    It's finally
        over.

Ding ding ding!

DUKE'S

Since we have some celebrating to do, we do the obvious thing and go for pie and mash.

'You want to come?' I ask Kwaku.

He scratches the back of his head, like he does when he's confused. 'What is it? Just pie and mash?'

I laugh. 'No, it's way more than that. Food of the gods, ain't it, Denny?' I nudge him in the side.

Denny pulls me in a headlock and ruffles my hair with the ball of his fist. 'Too right. I ain't had it for flippin' ages. I might get three pies.'

Seffi slaps Denny on the arm. 'You pig. Food of the bloomin' universe, more like.'

Kwaku shrugs. 'I'll give it a go, but I'm not convinced. I doubt it's better than hot wings. Now, that's the true food of the gods.'

We go for the big table at the back, cos, obviously, since the last time we were here at Albert's, our family is now a lot bigger. We're blended. Plus Kwaku, cos your best friend is definitely family too.

We shove onto the benches, tight together, our elbows digging into each other, and Hayden is in his buggy at the end.

Dad and Denny go to the counter to order. I wonder if they are mates again. I think about the last time we were in Albert's . . . How they'd rowed that day. That's when all the bad stuff started. I don't want that to happen again.

But I look closer – Kwaku's being all cute and doing nose-bib things with Hayden, Mum and Seffi are laughing about something.

Life is in motion.
Like a rhythm.
Like a beat.
Like one of Kwaku's raps.
Like boxing.

Albert is looking
down at us all from his
photo on the wall.
I wonder what his

life had been like.
Had his happy-looking
family had rubbish times?
Made up after big rows?
Added new members?

I'll never know,
but I guess so.

'Right, there you go, my little winner.' Dad puts a plate of double pie and mash in front of me. I slide it across the table to where Denny will be sitting when he comes back from the counter with my plate.

'What you doing?' Dad asks.

'Denny's, ain't it? I don't get double.'

'You do now,' Dad says with a cheeky grin. 'I'm proud of my girl, ain't I? You blimmin' deserve it.'

'At bleedin' last.' I pull the plate back towards me. 'Can I give Hayden some?' I ask Seffi.

'Well, he ain't eating yet. But a bit of liquor on his tongue won't hurt, I suppose.'

'It's only right his first proper grub is pie and mash,' says Denny.

'Too right.' I dip my finger in the liquor, put it on the baby's lips. He flicks his tongue out like a little lizard, scrunches his face up and smiles. 'He loves it. He's a proper cockney,' I say, proud as you like. Everybody cheers. Even the old girl behind the counter.

'You wait till you try wings,' whispers Kwaku, pushing the food around his plate. He doesn't look too impressed.

I give him a little dig in the leg. 'Don't you like it?'

'It's OK. But next time, I'll go without this weird green stuff.' He dribbles the liquor off his spoon, makes a funny face.

'Oh right, that's it – disown this boy, Molly,' says Dad, ribbing him.

I can see that sparkle
in Dad's eye that
Denny
told me he used to have.
He looks . . .
Happy.

The bell on the door rings as it opens, letting the cold winter breeze and buzz of traffic into the shop. It's Tiff. What's she doing here? She looks about, spots us, comes over.

'Thought you lot would be here.'

'That predictable, are we? Everything all right?' says Dad.

'Yeah, Rory, I'm pretty good. It's just . . . look, we just heard about old Frankie boy, and me and some of the lads have been trying to work out what to do about Duke's. We got into the safe, in Frank's office, and found paperwork. Turns out your name is still on the deeds. We really need someone to sort the place out. A lot of youngsters in there rely on the club to keep them out of trouble, an' I get that. If it wasn't for Duke's, I'd have probably ended up in the nick myself. So . . . I was wondering . . . well . . . we was wondering if we could drop these off with you.'

Tiff puts the keys to Duke's on the table in front of Dad.

Dad looks across at Mum, like he's never been so shocked. Mum almost spits out her tea. I notice Seffi whispering something in Denny's ear.

'You mean . . .' Dad picks up the keys, examines them like they are some sort of foreign object.

Tiff nods. 'It'll take a bit of doing up. Frank let it get in a right state. But we'll all help fix it up and, between us, we reckon we can scrape together some cash to improve it. You'd have to sign the paperwork, but . . . well, we really need you, mate.'

Dad shrinks back into himself. He looks scared. I'm scared he's gonna say no. That he'll go back to hiding under his duvet.

I jump up from my chair. 'Dad . . .' I pause. 'You can do it. I believe in you! Make a dream happen.'

Denny leans across, smiles at me, his dimples deeper than ever, holds my hand. 'Yeah, Dad, make a dream happen!'

Dad looks like he's going to cry. 'Help me run the place, son?'

Denny's halfway through munching a bite of pie. He gulps it down, almost chokes. 'Me? Serious? After everything I've done?'

I cross all my fingers and my toes in the hope that Denny will say yes.

'That was my fault, son. Let me make it up to you.' Dad puts his hand out to shake Denny's.

Denny looks at Mum, who smiles and nods, then he looks at Seffi, who smiles too. Then he looks at me. I punch him in the arm. 'Just say yes, div.'

Denny gets up and holds open his arms to Dad. 'All right, yeah. Let's do this!' They cuddle tight, pat each other's backs hard.

A proper man hug.

This has to be the best day of my live–long life. Winning my fight, getting Denny back, holding Hayden . . . and now Duke's.

'Looks like we've got some more celebrating to do!' says Dad. 'Let's get down the pub. Pints are on me.'

Everyone starts packing their stuff up and moving out.

But I don't move.

I look at Kwaku, he's still pushing his pie around in the green liquor, pouting.

'You coming, Molly?' says Denny.

'Nah, I promised Kwaku I'd help him with his footwork.'

'Huh?' says Kwaku.

Dad leans over, kisses me on the head. 'Proud of you – and I don't just mean the boxing neither. You done this family proud. You see all this?' He points behind him with his thumb to where everyone is smiling, laughing, excited. 'None of this would've happened without you.'

'Well, I can't take *all* the credit,' and I smile at Kwaku.

'All right, well, have a laugh training.' Dad leans down, plunges a fork into the last of his pie and stuffs it in his gob, then he legs it out the door, leaving me and Kwaku on our tod.

Kwaku turns to me. 'I don't need help with my footwork, cheeky git.'

'I know. I just thought we could hang out. Besides, you're probably hungry after not eating any of that green stuff. Wings?'

Happy Boy smiles, beams out of his face, like I'd just offered him a million pounds. 'Ooooh, yeah – wings!'

DING DING DING!

We've been to Dixy Chicken. Kwaku had fifteen wings and I just had a milk-shake, cos I was proper full up after double pie and mash. We laugh. Talk about our next fights. Talk about the fights we've had. I tell him that girls are better fighters than boys and how I am gonna be better than Nicola Adams one day, and he agrees.

We sit together in the middle of the boxing ring at Duke's, sharing a bag of Haribo. I look round the huge hall. It's sort of mine now.

A family business.

Kwaku fiddles with some gum in his mouth. 'Do you reckon Hayden might train here one day – take after his stepdaddy, after his auntie Molls?'

'God, that's ages off. But, yeah, I suppose. Maybe. It's in the blood, ain't it?'

'Certainly is. Hey, maybe we could train him. We'd be well old by then. Probably too past it to box ourselves.' He laughs like a moron at his own joke. Kwaku's always so happy. It's so nice being around the daft sod. Not many people have his ability to be so supportive and upbeat despite everything.

'I've been thinking though,' he continues, 'that maybe I might not be a boxer when I grow up.'

'Really? But what else would you be?'

Kwaku beams, taps his hand on his chest. 'Thinking about being a rapper, aren't I?'

'I think that's a great idea!'

It seems like as good a time as any. I shuffle closer to him and take the stone out of my pocket that I've had with me since that day on the bench. The day we decided to look for Denny together. The day that Kwaku showed me I should have faith in myself.

'I made you this cos you helped me, and Denny says you should always tell someone when they've done something good for you or the world. People need telling.' I put it in his hand.

He looks down at the stone and smiles his best Happy Boy smile and nods like crazy. Because now, written on the stone are the words

impossible is nothing.

And it is. As long as you have your people with you by your side, anything is possible.

ACKNOWLEDGEMENTS

I'd like to extend my never ending thanks to the following people:

My editor Harriet Birkinshaw and the amazing team at Flying Eye Books, for your guidance, patience and unwavering faith in me and this book.

Julia Churchill, my fabulous agent, for taking a huge shot on me. For the many phone calls and boosts along the way and for encouraging me to take risks with my writing, however unusual.

Super thanks to Tosin Akinkunmi and Justin Moore for the wonderful book jacket they have created together. A writer spends a lot of time imagining their first cover and this has surpassed my every dream.

The teachers and students from Bath Spa University's Writing for Young People MA. With special thanks to Steve Voake, who encouraged me to write this book and Elen Caldecott, my mentor.

Lesley Parr and Rebecca Moses-Paterson, my best writing buddies, thank you for your honesty, excitement for my writing and friendship. It wouldn't have been possible without you.

My first creative writing tutor, Maggie Butt, who has championed my writing for almost twenty years now. Where did the time go?

Andy, Betty, Chas and Meryl Duckhouse, for funding my dreams and the love, support and memories shared along the way.

My friends, David Mears, Meghan Havard and Rhysian Plant – for showing me the light on the dark days.

Mum and Dad, for filling my childhood with books and music and teaching me that I am capable of anything, if only I try my best. I am me, because of you.

For the everlasting awe and inspiration you all give me, my children, Jack, Pacey and Hazel.

The platonic love of my life, James (Jimi) Morgan. You see the real me and nurture my strength and soul, always with a compassionate heart. You are my Kwaku.